SUNRISE

SUNRISE

AL LAMANDA

FIVE STAR
A part of Gale, Cengage Learning

GALE
CENGAGE Learning®

Detroit • New York • San Francisco • New Haven, Conn • Waterville, Maine • London

GALE
CENGAGE Learning®

LIBRARY OF CONGRESS CATALOGING-IN-PUBLICATION DATA

Lamanda, Al.
    Sunrise : a John Bekker mystery / Al Lamanda. — First edition.
        pages cm
        ISBN 978-1-4328-2714-4 (hardcover) — ISBN 1-4328-2714-6
    (hardcover)
        I. Title.
    PS3612.A5433S85 2013
    813'.6—dc23
                                                                2013008274

First Edition. First Printing: July 2013
Find us on Facebook– https://www.facebook.com/FiveStarCengage
Visit our website– http://www.gale.cengage.com/fivestar/
Contact Five Star™ Publishing at FiveStar@cengage.com

Printed in Mexico
1 2 3 4 5 6 7 17 16 15 14 13

For Brenda. Without you this book never would have been written.

CHAPTER 1

The sun was barely up when the surfers took to the beach to ride the waves of a new tide. They wore black wetsuits and from a distance, they resembled seals bobbing on the crests.

Gulls complained and scavenged for scraps of food.

It was a cold morning, but I knew it would warm up quickly once the sun started to beat down on the sands.

I sipped coffee from a slightly chipped mug and lit the first cigarette of the day. Both tasted harsh, but after a few sips and puffs, things smoothed out nicely. For the past seven months or so, Janet had nagged me to quit smoking and I'd promised her that I would.

Just not today.

Probably not tomorrow.

Soon.

Wasn't that the smoker's pledge?

I can quit anytime I want to, I just don't want to today.

From the rusty lawn chair in front of my one-bedroom trailer on the beach, I watched the sun glimmer off the ocean as it rose higher in the sky and the surfers riding the cresting waves. It was turning out to be a beautiful morning. The air was crisp with a hint of the warmth that was to soon follow.

The lawn chair creaked under my weight.

Janet nagged me to replace it and I'd promised her I would.

Just not today.

Today was reserved for nothing. For every moment I was

awake today, my game plan was to do absolutely nothing. I hoped it would be everything I thought it would be.

As it turns out, doing nothing is more difficult than it sounds.

Nothing is the lack of something and things have a way of creating something from nothing all on their own.

From my trailer to the edge of town is a stretch of about five hundred yards of public beach. A sandy road that runs from that edge to my trailer and beyond is reserved for the Parks Department and lifeguard use, but nobody pays much attention to that law. Four-wheelers zoom by at all hours of the day and night, and rarely does anyone get a ticket because rarely is anyone paying attention.

What caught my attention was the white sheriff's cruiser that entered the beach and drove slowly across the sand. Even from fifteen hundred feet, there was no mistaking the distinct outline of the lights on the roof.

I searched my recent memory for somebody I'd offended.

That came up blank.

The cruiser came a bit closer.

Ten days ago, I took my daughter Regan to see the mouse in Florida. Janet, her son Mark and Sister Mary Martin accompanied us. We stayed a week in the mouse resort and had a great time.

Regan spoke her first word in nearly thirteen years.

That was a big day and a big deal for all of us.

Regan went mute at the age of five and for good reason.

I was a sergeant with Special Crimes back then. Mostly RICO crimes interested us. We ran an investigation that came to fruition after nearly two years of work involving Eddie Crist, the head of the East Coast mob. It was a team effort between the FBI and us. We had a witness, a middle management mob boss looking to deal his way out of life without parole by singing like a canary. Freedom and a new identity were worth more to him than his honor and thirty years.

A few days before Crist's trial was scheduled to begin, the witness and several FBI agents were killed when the safehouse they occupied blew up from a pound of C-4 explosives ignited by a Mercury switch on a timer.

The mark of a real pro.

That same day, a man broke into my home to deliver a message intended for me. I wasn't home. He delivered the message to my wife Carol instead. He raped and murdered her in our bed while our five-year-old daughter watched from her hiding place in the bathroom.

After Carol's funeral, I went into a decade-long tailspin where a quart of Scotch was my medication of choice. I lost my job, my daughter, sobriety and my life.

Carol's sister Janet did what she could. She sold our house, banked the profits in my name and helped me buy the trailer I still live in today.

Regan went into a home called Hope Springs Eternal, where they treat children suffering from traumatic shock.

I was drunk round the clock and didn't even know where the place was located. My visits were few and far between. My daughter was a reminder of what I'd had and lost, and I was a reminder of the horrific event she'd witnessed. Seeing each other did neither of us any good.

Or so I lied to myself.

Salvation, so to speak, came when the mobster I blamed for all my troubles came to my rescue.

Eddie Crist was dying of cancer. He had me kidnapped and forced me sober so he could hire me to find whoever murdered Carol. It seems that while I drank a decade away, many things happened I was unaware of.

Michael Crist, Eddie's son, was murdered in a mob-related war over territory control. Crist denied having anything to do with Carol's death, but suspected his son might have. Once sober, a real treat getting that way, Crist hired me to investigate and clear his son's name or prove his guilt.

Either way, Crist wanted to know.

He didn't want my wife on his conscience when he died, so he told me.

Turns out, it was Crist footing the eight grand a month bill for Regan's care and he arranged for it to continue after his death for as long as necessary. Crist, for all his brutal reputation, was old-fashioned mob. Civilians, especially women and children, were off-limits.

I took the job.

I found who murdered my wife.

It wasn't Michael Crist.

Eddie Crist died a much happier man.

For my services, I received a six-figure check.

And a second shot at life.

I spent twelve of those six figures in Florida. The need for Sister Mary Martin was genuine. The nun spent a dozen years by Regan's side in the home. Regan loved and trusted her above all else.

Even me.

Couple of things I discovered in Florida. One was that Regan, despite her silence and seeming handicap of traumatic shock, was capable of having fun. She bonded with Mark, Janet's son, and toward the end of the trip, she was acting like an older sister to the younger boy.

I also discovered my stomach turns on roller coasters and that Janet's does not. After one such ride when I was losing the ball of pink cotton candy I had just before boarding, Regan rubbed my back and called me Dad.

It came out soft and sweet, like she'd been saving it up just for that occasion since the age of five.

Maybe she had been?

Just that single word was enough to reduce me to a bawling mess of fatherly goo.

Home twenty-four hours, my plans to do nothing came to a quick end when the cruiser arrived and Sheriff Jane Morgan stepped out with a pastry box I recognized as belonging to Pat's Donut Shop.

"I have a long story to tell," Jane said.

"How long?" I said.

Jane rattled the box. "Three apiece and these ain't cheap."

"That long, huh?"

"Longer."

"I'll get us some fresh coffee," I said.

CHAPTER 2

I bit into a powdered lemon cream donut half the size of a hubcap and washed it down with a sip of coffee.

Jane did the same, but with a Boston cream. She sat in the rusty lawn chair usually reserved for my only neighbor, Oz.

I had powdered sugar on my fingers and licked it off.

I've known Jane about twenty years. She was a deputy for six years before running for County Sheriff, a position she's held for three six-year terms, soon to be four. Her department covers the small towns inside the county that don't have police departments. They also provide full coverage to the county jail. In all, Jane supervises one hundred and fifty-one deputies, plus an additional twenty-five during tourist season to handle the drunks and noise complaints.

She is a tough, fair and honest cop. She's also a wife and the mother of four sons, three of which are in college. I'm not sure which is harder, being a cop or a mother.

"So, what's the bribe for?" I said.

"Think of it as breakfast," Jane said.

"No one in their right mind would eat three of these sugar-loaded fat bricks for breakfast," I said.

"We're cops," Jane said. "Donuts are in our blood if not our waistline."

"You're a cop," I corrected her. "I'm a civilian ten years now."

"Bullshit. You're more cop now than ever. You just don't have a badge anymore. It's in your blood like the donuts."

"Jane, you didn't drive an hour to feed me donuts," I said. "Something's on your mind you want to dump on me, so you might as well go ahead and unload."

Jane removed her cap. Her shoulder-length blonde hair fell out. It made her blue eyes appear bluer. "Carly Simms," she finally said. "She's in the jackpot."

I looked my question to Jane.

"While you were playing with Mickey, I arrested her three nights ago."

"Carly Simms, the state prosecutor?" I said.

Jane nodded. "The one and the same."

I stared at her. "What for?"

"Murder One."

"Shit."

"Yeah."

"It didn't make the Florida news."

"It hasn't made the news period," Jane said. "I put a blackout on it until charges have been officially filed."

"Which is?"

"Four o'clock today."

"And how do you think that will go?"

"Evidence says murder one all the way."

"And me?"

"Let's talk about that."

"What?"

"That she, and I'll go along with it, wants to hire you to investigate and prove her innocent," Jane said.

"You're not serious?"

"As the heart attack my overweight slug of a husband will have any day now."

"Come on, Jane," I said. "What the hell can I do that the defense, prosecutor and your department can't?"

"Break the law, for one thing," Jane said. "We have to operate within its limits. Sort of. You, on the other hand, can do whatever the fuck you want. That gives you an edge. Plus, you're damn good and you know it."

"And if I find something that I came across illegally, what good does that do her in court?"

"Come on, Bekker," Jane said. "I'm not here to give you a hand job. I'm asking for your help."

"Since you put it so eloquently."

"I'll drive you to my office and show you everything we've got."

"Not so fast," I said. "Two things."

"What?"

"I realize you're her friend, but is that clouding your judgment a bit?"

"What kind of a fucking asshole question is that?" Jane snapped. "I arrested the bitch personally. I just happen to think she's innocent of the charges."

"Okay."

"What's the second thing?" Jane said.

"We finish these donuts first."

Jane looked in the box. Two remained.

"My waistline isn't going to like this," she said and picked up another Boston cream. "But, it's not exactly like I have to impress my husband anymore, do I?"

CHAPTER 3

The drive to Jane's office took about forty-five minutes, which is about fifteen minutes outside the city limits. She and her staff could enforce the law within a city or a township that does have a police department, provided there was just cause such as a bench warrant or if they were called in for backup by the local department.

Jane interpreted her boundaries loosely.

Another way to put that was that Jane did whatever she thought a situation warranted. I've seen her in action. She's not a woman I'd like to tangle with up close and personal, or from a distance either, for that matter.

I lit a cigarette and lowered my window.

Jane glared at me.

"You going to charge me with smoking?" I said.

"I was going to ask if you could spare one," Jane said.

I lit a second and passed it to her. She inhaled and blew smoke through her nostrils like a beautiful blonde dragon.

"So do I get any details on the way, or am I supposed to quietly take in the scenery?" I said.

"I'm better at show and tell," Jane said. "And I also hate repeating myself. Take in the scenery and shut up."

Jane drove. We both smoked. We arrived at the Public Safety Building where the County Sheriff's Office and holding jail was located. Someone was in Jane's reserved space. She parked in a handicapped spot and entered the building fuming.

I stayed two paces behind her.

The first one to feel Jane's wrath was the desk sergeant. He gave her an *uh-oh* look as she blasted through the front door and marched to the desk.

"Who the fuck is in my spot?" Jane all but roared.

"I can't see the lot from here, Sheriff," the desk sergeant said.

"Useless," Jane said. "Have the fucking thing towed. I don't care who it belongs to, have it hauled away. I'll be in a meeting with this mope next to me. Unless the ground opens up and swallows the building, hold my calls."

"Sure thing, Sheriff."

"And have somebody make a fresh pot of coffee and send it to my office," Jane said. "Bekker is a caffeine junkie."

The desk sergeant looked at me.

I shrugged innocently.

"Anything else, Sheriff?" the desk sergeant said.

"If you smell cigarette smoke, ignore it."

Jane's office occupied the rear of the second floor just down the hall from the detectives' and investigation units.

We entered and she closed the door.

"Conference table," Jane said.

Just as we sat, Jane's hard line phone rang. She went to answer it at her desk. "What?" she snarled.

"Sheriff," the desk sergeant said. "That car you want towed belongs to the Deputy County Commissioner. He's meeting with the . . ."

"I don't give a rat's ass who he is or who he's meeting with," Jane said. "He moves it right now or he picks it up later at the tow yard."

Jane hung up the phone, picked up a file from her desk, returned to the table and took the chair to my right.

There was a curt knock on the door. It opened and a deputy

came in with a serving tray. "You asked for coffee, Jane?" he said and placed the tray on the table.

The tray held a full pot, two mugs, sugar, cream and a small tin ashtray hidden under a napkin.

"Go fight some crime and make sure we aren't disturbed for at least one hour," Jane said. "Shoo."

The deputy nodded and left us alone.

Jane poured.

I lit two smokes.

Jane opened the file. "Read first before asking questions."

I read.

At 1:28 in the morning of Saturday last, Mrs. Susan Atkins in Room 13 at the Peek A Boo Motel off Route 126 placed a 911 call that was received by the County Sheriff's Department. Mrs. Atkins and her husband, Shaun, were woken up by a thumping noise coming through the wall of Room 15.

At 1:44 in the morning, a cruiser arrived on the scene with two deputies. After knocking on the door of Room 15 failed to get a response, a deputy went to the manager's residence on site, woke the manager and obtained a room key.

Upon entering Room 15, the deputies found the body of Jon Cecil Hughes, age listed as twenty-three, on his back on the rug with a ten-inch long, brass letter opener lodged in his chest. He had been stabbed three times total, the last one taking dead aim through the breastplate into the heart.

Hughes had a blood alcohol level of 2.1, according to his autopsy report.

Carly Ann Simms, age listed as forty-four, was found passed out on the bed. She was naked and covered in blood. Her blood alcohol level was listed at 2.6. She remained unconscious for several hours and awoke in a hospital bed without memory of stabbing Hughes, although her prints were the only set found on the murder weapon.

Simms gave statements to Sheriff Jane Morgan at the hospital where Morgan placed Simms under arrest for Murder One pending arraignment.

According to Simms's statement, she stopped at the Watering Hole Bar for a drink after a particularly difficult day at the office. Cases were piling up, manpower was short, and a drink was called for. She took a seat at the bar and ordered a glass of white wine. Hughes was seated alone at the other end of the bar. When Simms finished her glass, before she paid the bill and left, Hughes had a full glass of wine sent to her seat. This led to that and several hours later, they found themselves in Room 15 at the Peek A Boo Motel.

Simms stated that she had no memory of an argument with Hughes or of stabbing him. She remembered the full bottle of white wine they purchased on the way to the room and identified the letter opener as one belonging to her and that she carried in her purse. She also stated that until that evening, she never met or spoke with Hughes on any level.

I refilled the mugs and lit fresh smokes for each of us.

"Not much of a statement to work with," I said.

Jane blew smoke out of her nostrils. "No."

"The Atkinses?"

"They saw nothing," Jane said. "The thumping they heard, they couldn't identify. It could have been Hughes hitting the floor."

"How did they get from the bar to the motel?" I said. "There's no mention of a car parked at the motel."

"Mystery," Jane said. "A rental belonging to Hughes was still parked at the Watering Hole, as is the Taurus belonging to Simms."

"How far is the bar from the motel?"

"Four and a third miles."

"What time did the bartender say they left?"

"Nine-thirty, a little later."

"Cab?"

"We're working on that," Jane said. "Nothing so far."

"Maybe it was gypsy or off the meter?"

"Maybe. The bartender remembers them leaving together, but couldn't see if they got a cab or not."

"Four miles and drunk, they didn't walk."

"Very unlikely."

"What about the manager of the motel?"

"He said they arrived at ten," Jane said. "He locks the office at ten and they walked in just as he was closing up for the night. He stated they were a bit drunk, but so was everyone else at the motel. It's a cheat-on-your-spouse kind of a place. Nobody looks anybody in the eye. We took a call last year when a man checked in to meet a woman he found on the Internet that turned out to be his wife. He killed her in a rage, and then killed himself by placing a plastic bag over his head."

"What do you got on Hughes?"

"I'll give you copies of everything," Jane said. "But all we know so far is, he's from Utah, worked for a computer designer company as a design engineer and was here for a meeting with a client."

"He's only twenty-three."

"Which is like forty in the computer field," Jane said. "He graduated college with a degree in computer science at twenty-one and went to work for the design company where he worked his way up the ladder to middle management within two years."

"I can barely click the mouse," I said.

"It's a brave new world, Bekker," Jane said.

"Time of death and all that other bullshit?"

"About the same time as the thumping sounds heard by the Atkinses," Jane said. "Cause of death is the letter opener to the heart."

"Crime scene photos?"

Jane stood up and crossed her office to the desk. When she returned, she held dozens of photographs that she laid out on the table.

I lit two fresh smokes and we studied the photographs.

I'd seen better.

I'd seen worse.

I'd seen just about everything there is to see in a crime scene photo.

However, never had I seen a collection of crime scene photographs that so clearly spelled out the guilt for the defendant.

"What are you thinking?" Jane said.

"Most of the blood is on the bed. Very little is on the floor. He was stabbed twice on the bed before the fatal stab, then rolled to the floor where he died."

"The thumping?"

"Probably. Could have been Simms hitting the wall before she passed out."

I looked at the photographs of Simms taken by the two deputies first on the scene. Usually, photographs aren't taken until after homicide and forensics arrive, but Jane said they didn't know if Simms would wake up and disturb evidence, so they clicked away to preserve the moment.

Simms was on her back next to a deep pool of dry blood that appeared almost black. She was passed out cold. A stream of blood covered her right arm. Spotted specks of blood covered the back of her left hand.

"Besides the fact that she has an ass, legs and a rack I would kill for, what does this photo tell you?" Jane said.

"That's she's guilty," I said.

Jane looked at me.

"What does it tell you?" I said.

"That she's passed out drunk," Jane said. "That she works out a lot to keep that body the way it is at forty-four. The empty wine bottle on the floor tells me they were absolutely shitfaced, verified by the blood tests. What it doesn't tell me is if they had sex and that she positively murdered Jon Hughes."

"Jon Cecil Hughes," I said.

"Cecil," Jane said. "Who gives a kid Cecil for a middle name?"

"Yuppies. What did the lab reports say about sex?"

"None. Her honey pot was clean," Jane said. "No traces of semen on his little dinky, the bed or anywhere else."

"So they sat around drinking wine for three and a half hours, then she just decided to stab him to death with her letter opener?" I said.

"How about this?" Jane said. "They both passed out drunk and woke up hours later. Simms didn't know where she was or who she was with, panicked and killed him in what she thought was self-defense."

"She doesn't say that in her statement."

"She doesn't say shit in her statement," Jane said. "I'm just throwing it out to see if it sticks."

"It doesn't," I said. "What does the evidence tell you?"

"She's guilty."

"So does the photo," I said. "See the trail of blood on her right arm. She's right handed. As she stabbed down, blood squirted up, then ran down her arm while still wet. See the specks of blood on the palm of her left hand. That's a defensive blood pattern, caused by holding your hand visor-like to shield your eyes from spray. As she stabbed down, she protected her eyes."

"Fuck," Jane said. "And the prosecutors will see that, too."

"Maybe they won't, but the experts they hire to examine the photos sure will," I said.

"And give testimony to the fact in court."

"No doubt," I said. "However, the judge will see this as a conflict of interest, seeing as how the prosecutors trying the case work for the defendant. He'll move the trial out of the county."

"And my jurisdiction," Jane said.

"I've known you a long time, Jane," I said. "Since your college-age sons were in first grade and kindergarten. I've never known you to compromise evidence or an arrest."

"And I'm not now, you donut-eating jack-off," Jane said. "I don't want to influence the prosecutor, the defense or the evidence. Not even you. I just don't believe she's guilty."

"Why?"

"My gut," Jane said and grabbed her middle between two fingers. "Which is about four inches larger than it was pre three donuts."

"Can we see her?" I said.

"No problem."

CHAPTER 4

Carly Simms wore the standard female prison garb of county lockup. A drab dress and slippers. I didn't know what underwear was provided to women or if they were allowed to wear their own. My guess was not. Some women would kill for Victoria's Secret low-cut thongs.

So I've been told.

Her shoulder-length black hair was in a short ponytail. She wore no makeup and in the harsh lighting, the forty-four-year-old wrinkles and creases around her eyes were evident, but not unattractive.

The puffy bags from lack of sleep did her no justice, but I doubted her looks were a major concern to any of us at the moment.

She wasn't cuffed to the steel loop on the table. I slid my pack of cigarettes and a container of coffee across, then took a seat. Jane sat next to me. We each had coffee and I slid the tin ashtray to the center of the table.

Simms grabbed the cigarette pack, lit one, blew smoke through her nose and glared at me.

"Are you sober?" Simms said.

"You're not in a position to bark questions like that at me," I said.

"But are you?" Simms said.

"Eight months without a drop," I said. "Did you kill that man?"

"How long have we known each other, Bekker?" Simms said.

"Off and on, a long time," I said. "That doesn't mean you didn't stab that man through the heart with your letter opener."

"No, it doesn't," Simms said as she ignored the ashtray and flicked the cigarette ash onto the floor. "But I didn't."

"Your statement says that you can't remember," I said. "So how do you know that you didn't?"

Simms stared at me.

I stared at Simms.

Jane looked at both of us.

"I'm missing something here," Jane said. "I thought you wanted to hire Bekker to investigate and report to your lawyer. Why are you busting his balls?"

"We're just setting the ground rules," I said.

"To establish what?" Jane said.

"Whether or not I'm being honest with him," Simms said.

"Are you?" Jane said.

"She is if she answers my question," I said.

"What question?" Jane said.

Simms took a sip of coffee, another hit off the cigarette, then said, "The answer is, Bekker, because I'm a complete fraud."

"Unless you tell me you're secretly a man, I don't follow you," I said.

"What's my reputation, Bekker?" Simms said.

"Tough as nails, straight shooter, a prosecutor who never gives a criminal a break," I said. "And man-eater."

"Most of my staff hates my guts," Simms said. "I started as a junior DA eighteen years ago and clawed my way to the top by being tougher, meaner and harder than all the men I worked with. A complete bitch. I had to. I didn't have the advantage of being born with a set of balls as a stepping-stone. Most women who enter the DA or State's Office drop out within three years to have babies or go into some soft private practice firm. I happen to like public service and wanted to stay there, but not as a fetch-me-my-coffee junior DA. So I had to invent super-bitch to compete with the men. My staff is mostly male. Like I said, they hate my guts."

"Oh my," Jane said. "What a mouthful."

"Which didn't answer my question," I said.

"I didn't kill Jon Hughes because it's not in me to do so," Simms said. "Underneath the super-bitch image is a woman who is afraid of spiders in the bathtub. Even blind drunk, I couldn't and wouldn't do something like that."

"How do you explain the evidence that says otherwise?" I said.

"I can't," Simms said. "I'm hoping hiring you will."

"What if the evidence I find says that you're guilty?" I said.

"I'm willing to take that chance," Simms said. "Because I know that I'm not."

I looked at Jane. "You said four o'clock the story breaks."

"And all hell around here with it," Jane said.

"Who's defending you?" I asked Simms.

"Charles Gibson from the Public Defender's office," Simms said. "My staff will have a field day with his doughy ass."

"Not anymore," I said.

"Bekker, I draw a public servant's salary," Simms said. "Sixty-eight thousand last year. Minus taxes, pension, insurance, mortgage, car payments and everything else, I have to use my life savings to pay you. Even if I'm found innocent, my career is over. Even in the private sector, who is going to hire a forty-four-year-old bitch that lures young men into hotel rooms and who, despite an innocent verdict, might still be guilty?"

"That's your problem," I said. "My problem will be to help your lawyer prove your innocence in court."

"What lawyer are you talking about?" Simms said.

"The one I'll be back with in a couple of hours," I said. "Be prepared to be scraped down to the bone, because that's the only way this will work. Any bullshit and he walks and I go with him. Deal?"

The look of fear in her eyes when Simms nodded told me all I needed to know. She was too scared to lie and play games with me.

That was a good thing.

I stood up from the table.

"Jane, I'll be back in a couple of hours," I said. "Can you have a deputy drive me home?"

"No problem," Jane said. "Maybe you could pick up some more of those donuts on the way back for the boys at the desk?"

Simms cocked her head at me. "Pat's?"

I looked at Jane. "She allowed?"

"Oh, what the fuck," Jane said.

CHAPTER 5

Back in my trailer, I changed into a suit minus the tie, then walked the half mile to town where I keep my seven-year-old Marquis in a parking lot that charges by the month.

The drive to the law office of Lewis and Clark and Associates took about forty minutes. It was downtown and located on the top floor of a luxury office building. Lewis and Clark represented Eddie Crist, mob boss of the East Coast. Their retainer fees started at six figures and went up from there, but that's what a top-dog criminal defense firm costs these days. Lewis died a while back. David Clark was now top dog.

An appointment to see Clark could take weeks or even months. I didn't need an appointment. Clark owed me. When my wife was killed and my witness murdered, Clark arranged for the polygraph tests administered to Crist's circle, including his son, to be falsified. I uncovered that little nugget while employed by Crist and have kept it in my back pocket for you never know.

You never know was right now. I told the receptionist in the lavish lobby I was here to see Clark, I didn't have an appointment, but if you told him I was here, he'd be happy to see me right away.

He wasn't happy, but he saw me right away, anyway.

David Clark could have written the definition for the word *slick*. From his three thousand dollar suit, his five hundred dollar haircut, and his Trump-like office, the man reeked slick from every pore in his body.

"How long has it been, six months?" Clark said from behind his polished-to-a-sheen desk.

"Closer to eight," I said as I sat down in a leather chair that cost more than my Marquis did.

"And how is your daughter?"

"Not why I'm here," I said. "Why I am here is, I need you to represent somebody and I need you to do it right now and for free."

Clark looked at me as if I had something on the bottom of my shoe that smelled really bad. "Now why would I want to do that?" he said.

"Because if you don't, I will make it public knowledge that you faked polygraph tests to the courts and all those mobsters, rock stars and Hollywood types you keep on six-figure retainers will dump you and hire the old cowboy lawyer with the ponytail in Wyoming you always see when some celebrity murders their spouse."

"You'd have a great deal of difficulty proving that," Clark said.

"I don't have to," I said. "I just have to sort of mention it and it will grow wings."

Clark sighed. "You said somebody. Who is the somebody?"

"Carly Simms."

"The state prosecutor?"

"That got your interest, didn't it?" I said. "I'll tell you about it on the drive."

"You're not still driving that old . . ."

"Marquis, and yes, I am."

"We'll take my car."

"Can we stop for donuts on the way?" I said.

CHAPTER 6

Simms appeared a bit more rested on my second visit to the interrogation room. Jane had coffee and water brought in before we got started. I set a bag of four donuts on the table for Simms to take back to her cell later. Clark invoked client/attorney privilege and asked that Jane leave the room.

"Not Bekker," Simms said. "He works for me and he'll need to know everything I have to say if he's going to help. Besides, he brought me donuts."

"This won't be pretty," Clark said. "It can't be if I'm to do my job, and the prosecutor will do the same."

"You're talking to the prosecutor," Simms said. "I know exactly how it's going to be, right now and in court. Bekker stays."

Clark looked at me.

"Sure," I said. "No problem."

Clark used a legal pad and a digital tape recorder to note the meeting. The first hour was devoted to professional questioning. What cases were on her desk? How many? Motives of those being prosecuted? Prior enemies? Anybody with an ax to grind? Recently released ex-cons? That sort of thing.

"I will have my office request from your office discovery on whatever I deem pertinent to your defense," Clark said.

"They won't make it easy," Simms said. "I'm not what you would call well liked by my staff."

"Well liked has got nothing to do with it," Clark said. "They will do as I ask or I can arrange for some really bad things to occur that won't be fun on the receiving end."

"I won't ask what that means," Simms said.

"End of phase one," Clark said. "Let's move on to phase two. Understand this, your career as a prosecutor is over. If I can swing a not guilty or even a mistrial, you'll never work as an attorney in this state again, even if your license isn't revoked. So, you have no reason to lie or hold back any information from me."

Clark paused and followed Simms's eyes as she looked at me.

"Us," he corrected himself.

"Agreed," Simms said.

"Ever been married?" Clark said.

"No."

"Engaged?"

"Twice. Once when I was twenty-four, the second time when I was twenty-nine. Neither stuck. Neither did I."

"Boyfriends or relationships at present?"

"No."

"Are you a lesbian?"

"No."

"You're forty-four, very attractive and have no men in your life. Why is that?"

"I work sixty, seventy hours a week. That doesn't leave much time for fostering relationships," Simms said. "Or much else."

Clark flipped through pages of police reports.

"This bar . . . The Watering Hole, are you a regular?"

"It's on my way home. Sometimes after a bad day, I stop by for a glass of wine."

"How often?"

"On average about twice a week."

"Besides Mr. Hughes, have you ever picked up other men there?"

"Sometimes, not often."

"Give me a number."

Simms looked at me. I pulled out my cigarettes and lighter and slid them across the table. She lit one, inhaled smoke, thought.

"Say for the past year," Clark said.

Simms blew smoke as she thought. "Maybe five other times."

"With Mr. Hughes, that makes six. Is that correct?"

"Yes."

"Are they always young like Mr. Hughes?"

"Let me answer that with a question," Simms said. "How old are you, Mr. Clark?"

"Fifty-seven," Clark said.

"Are you married?"

"Yes."

"Say you weren't and you went into a bar looking for some female company," Simms said. "Are you going to talk to the women your own age, or are you going to seek out the youngest, prettiest woman who will pay attention to you?"

"That's pretty good," Clark said. He jotted a note. "We'll use that line on the stand if it comes to that."

"As long as I'm baring my soul to the bone here, what else do you want to know?" Simms said. "Do I pick up these men just for a one-night stand? For a quick fuck without strings or attachments? The answer is yes. It's simpler and easier than trying to find someone and maintain a relationship when you know you'll barely ever see them."

"About Mr. Hughes, have you ever met him prior to last Saturday?"

"No."

"How did the meeting between you two come about?"

"I stopped in for a glass of wine after twelve hours at the office," Simms said. "I had the one glass and was ready to leave when a second glass arrived at the bar. He initiated contact by buying me a drink."

"Did he say why?"

"He said he thought I had great legs."

"Then what happened?"

"We had several more glasses of wine and . . ."

"Several meaning what?"

"Honestly, I don't know," Simms said. "A lot, I would guess, judging from my condition when I awoke."

Clark flipped pages in the police reports, paused and read.

"Six each according to the bartender," Clark said. "At six ounces a glass."

"That's a lot."

"After that, what happened?"

"I have no idea."

"Do you remember who suggested a room at the Peek A Boo Motel?"

"No."

"Do you know how you arrived there?"

"No."

"Do you remember if you had sex with Mr. Hughes?"

"No."

"Do you remember killing Mr. Hughes?"

"No."

"Was anybody else in the room with you and Mr. Hughes?"

"No."

"Are you positive?"

"No, I'm not," Simms admitted. "I was too drunk to remember how I arrived at the motel. I was too drunk to remember if we had sex or not. I'm sure I was too drunk to know or remember if someone else was in the room before, during or after I passed out."

"But is it likely?"

"No, it is not."

"Why did you have the letter opener in your purse?" Clark said. "That strikes me as a bit unusual."

"I have a lot of stuff in my purse. I carry the letter opener because I don't want to ruin a fifty-dollar nail job when I open my mail. I don't leave it at my desk because it would get stolen by one of my juniors just to piss me off and a brass letter opener like that one cost twenty-five dollars."

Clark motioned and Simms showed him her perfect nails.

"Ever think of using the letter opener as a weapon?"

"No."

"Are you sure?"

"Yes. I carry a Smith and Wesson .32 caliber revolver for a weapon."

"Wait," I said.

Simms and Clark looked at me.

"There is no mention of a revolver belonging to you in any police report," I said. "Not one word."

Clark flipped pages.

"The contents of your purse make no mention of a revolver," Clark said. "And no mention of one at the scene is recorded."

"I know I had it when I left the office," Simms said. "I empty it and lock it in my desk when I arrive. I reload it and put it in my purse when I leave. That's my normal routine and I never vary it."

"You're licensed?" Clark said.

"Of course I'm licensed."

"I'll have your desk searched just in case you forgot it that day."

"I didn't forget it," Simms said. "It was Saturday. The office was empty except for a few. It's not located in the best neighborhood."

"Nonetheless. Do you know the serial number on the weapon?"

"It's written down in my house. The desk in the study. It's also on file at the gun store where I purchased it."

"I'll get it," I said.

Clark nodded, then turned and looked Simms in the eye. "I'll ask this only once. Did you kill that man?"

"No."

"No you can't remember, or no you didn't kill him?"

"No I can't remember," Simms admitted.

"Stabbing him?"

"I can't remember."

"Did you fight, have an argument?"

"No, I can't remember."

"Did you have sex?"

"No."

"You can't remember that you had sex, you remember that you didn't, or the medical reports tell you that you didn't?"

"I don't remember and I know I didn't because I was examined at the hospital."

"Other than what's in the reports, what do we know about Mr. Hughes?"

"Nothing," I said.

Simms closed her eyes for a moment as if thinking.

"Carly?" I said.

She opened her eyes. "I do remember one thing. We took our clothes off. Mr. Hughes was not what you would call well endowed."

I took a sip of my coffee and thought about that.

"Maybe you can try to remember other details more pertinent to the cause at hand?" Clark said. "Doesn't matter what they are, just so long as you remember them."

Simms nodded.

"What time is the announcement?"

"Four o'clock," I said.

"I'll make a statement after the prosecutor's office does," Clark said. "Bekker, you disappear. It's best for the defense if you're a ghost for a while."

"Sure," I said.

"Simms, you don't mention him, either," Clark said. "To no one."

"Not a problem," Simms said.

"I've got a couple of hours to prepare," Clark said. "Maybe the sheriff has an office I can use."

Clark and I stood up.

"Can I see Bekker alone for a moment?" Simms said.

Clark nodded and left the interrogation room.

Simms and I stared at each other.

It was on the tip of her tongue.

"Thank you, Bekker," Simms finally said.

"Well, that must have hurt," I said.

CHAPTER 7

"You pull a million-dollar lawyer out of your ass and he agrees to defend Simms and work for free," Jane said. "The least I could do is buy you lunch."

"The least I could do is let you," I said.

Jane drove us to a diner twenty minutes from her office. I noticed when we left that her cruiser was parked in her reserved spot. I didn't ask what happened to the deputy commissioner's car that occupied it earlier.

The diner was civilian, meaning it wasn't a cop hangout. She chose it so we could talk freely without being scrutinized by any of her deputies on break.

I ordered a well-done burger with bacon, a side order of onion rings and a cherry Coke. Jane went with the chef's salad and iced tea.

"What do we know about Jon Hughes?" I said as I bit into my burger. "Besides that he's dead."

"Just what you read," Jane said. "I have a detective doing a fact finding on him."

"The reports claim he registered into the room fifteen hours before he met Simms and for three days," I said. "His business trip?"

"Apparently."

"Find anything in the rental or Simms's Taurus?"

"Nothing useful like a .32 revolver," Jane said.

"Can we check out Room 15?" I said.

"After the press conference."

"Tomorrow morning, then," I said. "I'm having dinner with my daughter at six and I can't be late."

"Ten okay?"

"Fine."

"Give me your gut and your head."

"Everything in my head tells me she killed that man, even if she doesn't remember it," I said. "Everything in my gut is screaming she's innocent."

"Too bad guts can't sit on a jury."

"They do," I said. "All twelve of them."

"You know somebody is going to ask how a state's attorney can afford David Clark's fees," Jane said.

"And I'm sure Clark will have a prepared answer for that question."

Jane nodded and nibbled a bit of her salad. "One thing we haven't talked about," she said as she sipped iced tea. "Our state is a death penalty state."

"It's bad luck to talk about it," I said. "Like reminding a pitcher between innings he's throwing a no-hitter."

"I can't remember the last time this state executed a woman," Jane said.

"1958," I said. "She murdered her three children by giving them sleeping pills and then shot her husband with a 12-gauge. She was upset over the Christmas tree he picked out and the way the kids decorated it."

Jane nibbled a bit more salad.

I bit into the burger.

We looked at each other.

We both knew a trial instead of a plea could wind up with Simms on the death row jackpot tier.

"I'd like a ride home if you can swing it," I said.

"You don't want to witness the press conference of the

decade?" Jane said.

"My daughter gets very upset if I'm late," I said. "I'll catch it later on the news. I'm sure cable will run with it around the clock."

Jane nodded. "I'm glad things between you and Regan are working out."

"Me too," I said.

Chapter 8

I picked up Janet and Mark at her house and we drove straight to the Hope Springs Eternal complex. We arrived ten minutes early. On the drive, Mark filled me in on his curve ball and cutter, two pitches I had given him instruction on in the past six months. He said he could clock seventy-three miles an hour on the cutter, seventy-one on the curve ball.

Mark's voice starts to crack when he gets excited. He was still a scrawny kid, but had gained ten pounds since I came into his life. It wouldn't be too long before he would want to shave the peach fuzz he thought was growing on his chin.

"My second year in high school, I'm trying out for the team," Mark said, his voice crackling with teenage hormones.

"We have to enroll you in your first year first," Janet said. "Unless you think your grades are good enough to start out as a sophomore?"

"I'm just saying," Mark said. "That's my plans."

"Your plans are good grades or no baseball," Janet said. "Or anything else."

"Aw, Ma," Mark said.

"Aw, Ma, nothing," Janet said. "And I mean nothing."

I cast a glance her way. A grin crossed her lips. Months short of her forty-seventh birthday, Janet retained her youthful figure with daily three-mile jogs and a diet only a nurse could tolerate. She splurged during the weeks Mark stayed with his father Clayton and I stayed with her. I'm not a nurse and lettuce salads with oil and vinegar don't cut it for me. We compromise. A little salad with a steak goes a long way in the peace and harmony department.

At the gates of Hope Springs Eternal, a security guard checked us in and I parked in a visitor's spot in front of the main living quarters. Regan and Sister Mary Martin met us in the lobby.

At eighteen, my daughter is a slight bird of a girl and every bit as beautiful as her mother was in life. Wearing stylish jeans, a teal sweater and one-inch heels, Regan could have been the star at her senior prom if our lives had taken a different direction.

Sister Mary Martin wore civilian clothing, a below-the-knee, simple black dress with basic pumps. Her close-cropped hair was speckled with gray, but her blue eyes sparkled with youth and energy. The nun has raised my daughter since the age of five and she and Regan have an unbreakable bond of trust and love.

"I'm afraid she's being rather difficult," Sister Mary Martin said.

Regan shot the nun a *who me?* look.

"She has her mind set on a burger, fries and milkshake," the nun added.

"Works for me," Mark said.

"Me, too," I said.

"Don't encourage him," Janet said to me.

"A boy has to eat," I said. "And so does a man."

Regan gave me her *what about me?* look.

"And a girl," I quickly added.

We settled on the family-style burger joint a few miles from the complex and settled into a booth for six. Since returning from Florida, Regan has been allowed her own room in the complex, a major stride on her part. She also was given permission to keep and care for Molly, the stray cat who adopted me last year. Father Tomas, the psychiatrist who supervises Regan, said learning to care for something other than herself was a giant leap he didn't think was possible just a year ago.

Regan feeds Molly, changes the litter box twice a day and they sleep together on the full-size bed. The cat accompanies Regan on her walks in the garden. Tomas suggested Regan and Molly visit some of the younger children the way cats and dogs are used in nursing homes for therapy.

Sister Mary Martin told us about that at dinner.

Regan seemed very pleased with the idea.

"Can I see her later after dinner?" Mark said.

Regan nodded.

Janet squeezed my hand under the table.

An hour and a half later, Regan, Mark and Sister Mary Martin went up to Regan's room to see Molly.

Janet and I took an after-dark walk through the gardens away from the complex where I could smoke unseen.

"Couldn't wait for one of those, could you," Janet chastened me as she took my free hand.

"I'm working on quitting," I said.

"How is it you managed to quit drinking cold turkey after a ten-year binge, but those little white sticks kick your ass?"

"You know how on the weeks Mark stays with Clayton and I sleep over," I said. "And you wake up at three in the morning and go on a cookie raid, then complain how those last five pounds just won't come off. It's like that."

Janet showed me her sheepish grin. "You know about those, huh?"

"After all, I am a detective," I said. "And cookie crumbs and empty milk glasses in the sink are a clue."

We reached the darkest part of the gardens where a bench faced a lily pond.

"Want to make out?" Janet said. "Mark doesn't visit Clayton

for four more days, it's all you're gonna get."

"It's detention if we get caught," I said.

We were about to sit when a noise to our left caught our attention. It was Father Tomas. He stopped short and looked at the glowing red tip of the cigarette in my right hand.

"That should be good for some demerits," Janet said.

"Can you spare one of those?" Tomas said.

Janet rolled her eyes in the dark. I couldn't see it, but I felt her glare on my back as I took a step forward and gave the priest a cigarette and my lighter.

He lit up and handed me back the lighter.

"The spirit of God is very willing, the flesh of man is very weak," Tomas said. "And these are just too damn good to give up."

"That's what I say," I said.

"So much for Divine intervention," Janet said.

"Can we sit for a minute?" Tomas said. "I'd like to speak with you about Regan."

We sat on the bench, Janet on my left, Tomas to hers.

"I've discussed it at length with my colleagues and have asked them to evaluate Regan's case," Tomas said. "We feel that if she continues to show marked improvement in the next six months, Regan can live with you on a permanent basis. It would be with the stipulation that you have a home and not that trailer you live in, and that she receive in-home supervision while you work. Mr. Crist's generous support will more than cover the costs of Sister Mary Martin's daily commute to your home when you need to leave for work. I'll be honest. I never thought I would see that day, but we feel it's arriving rather quickly."

I stared at the priest.

"No drinking, of course," Tomas said. "Otherwise, I recommend it for Regan's continued progress and growth. The next step, so to speak. I'll continue to see her weekly on an outpatient basis here and at your home."

I nodded.

I stood up and walked away from the bench into the darkness of the gardens.

"Mr. Bekker?" Tomas called out to me.

I didn't respond and kept walking.

"Mr. Tough Guy doesn't want you to see him crying," I heard Janet say.

CHAPTER 9

While Mark got ready for bed, Janet and I watched the press conference held by the State Prosecutor's office, followed by a statement made by David Clark. Even though the conference was held six hours ago, there was no problem finding it on cable news.

I skipped the panel of experts giving their opinion and we took coffee in the backyard, leaving the floodlights off.

We sat in chairs facing the darkest part of the night sky so we could watch the stars unobstructed.

The house rule of no smoking while Mark was in the house was in effect. I settled for the coffee.

"So that's the case you're working on," Janet said.

"Yes."

"She's rather striking looking," Janet said and looked at me.

"She's okay," I said and looked at her.

"Why did she ask for you?"

"I've known her for almost twenty years or more," I said. "She tried many a case of mine and with great success, I might add."

"She looks guilty to me."

"That was file footage," I said. "Probably two years old."

"And you'll have to work closely with her?"

"Her lawyer," I said. "I probably won't see her but once or twice more."

Janet sighed openly. "Listen to me," she said. "I sound like a jealous girlfriend in high school."

"Would you wear my varsity sweater?" I said.

"Only if you wear my pin." Janet paused. "Neither of us is that old. How do we know this stuff?"

"Maybe we're just kidding ourselves."

"Who's not old?" Mark said as he came up behind us.

"Me," Janet said. "Your Uncle Jack is the Ancient Mariner."

"Does he play for Seattle?" Mark said.

"No, wise guy," Janet said. "Now say goodbye to your uncle and go to bed. He has a busy day tomorrow fighting crime and saving the lives of beautiful damsels in distress."

Mark looked at me. "What's she talking about?"

"When you get a bit older, you'll come to realize that you will never know what women are talking about," I said.

"Does that go for moms, too?"

"Especially moms."

"I'm going to count to ten," Janet said. "Starting with nine."

"I'm gone," Mark said and dashed back to the safety of the house.

"You, too. Go home," Janet said to me.

"Are you going to stay mad at me for doing my job?"

"I'm being silly again, aren't I?" Janet said. "And selfish, given the news about Regan tonight."

"That's something we need to talk about at another time," I said. "I'll call you tomorrow."

I stood up.

When I went to kiss Janet, she gave me her cheek, her little message that she wasn't pleased about my case.

Talking about or thinking, I told myself as I walked to the Marquis.

CHAPTER 10

I made a pot of coffee, turned on the floodlight outside my trailer and took a seat in the lawn chair to read Jane's reports. As I read the first page, I fiddled with an unlit cigarette.

Jon Cecil Hughes was given the name by Catholic Brothers at the Sacred Heart Orphanage located thirty miles southwest of Provo, Utah. According to Jane's research, Hughes received a first-rate education at the orphanage and left at eighteen to enter Salt Lake City Community College where he studied computer science. His rent, tuition and living expenses were paid for partially by the state, with the orphanage picking up the tab for the rest until the age of twenty-two or graduation. He worked some part-time jobs for extra spending money.

With Salt Lake CC being a two-year college, he transferred to Brigham Young University in Provo for two additional years. He graduated at the age of twenty-one and went to work for TRAX Inc., a small computer design company that specializes in video games. His plane ticket and meeting agenda for last week was with a video game company that hired him to create graphics and audio for a new game. Jane interviewed the man, Harold Mitchell, who claimed Hughes never showed for the meeting.

Until the four o'clock press conference this afternoon, Hughes was missing in action and generally unknown.

Not a lot of information to build a case around.

I went inside for a coffee refill, a pen and a notepad.

I sat and sniffed the unlit cigarette.

I started making notes.

Why was Hughes an orphan? That had nothing to do with his death, but it was a loose end in the investigation so far as contact information was concerned.

He wasn't married. Did he have a girlfriend? Was his drunken behavior and picking up Simms in a bar common behavior, or just a kid cutting loose?

Did he have enemies? That is, competitors in the computer industry? Did any of them stand to gain large profits by his murder? Such as contracts, money, promotions?

I held the unlit cigarette under my nose. I put it down on the card table next to my chair to resist the temptation of lighting it.

What could Hughes have said/done to Carly Simms to warrant such anger that she would stab him through the heart with a letter opener?

What happened to the .32 revolver? Did Simms lose it in transit to the room? Did she lose it at the bar? It wasn't used to murder Hughes, so disposing of it was unnecessary.

His driver's license listed Hughes as six foot one, two hundred and five pounds.

Simms weighed one thirty-five.

She's forty-four.

He's twenty-three.

Even drunk, how did Simms overpower Hughes to the point she could stab him?

Was Simms awake and Hughes passed out?

That was a strong possibility.

Besides the thump, did anyone hear arguing, screaming, fighting, anything?

I picked up the cigarette and placed it unlit between my lips. The thing about being a recovering drunk is that you miss the drinking, but you don't miss the way it makes you feel afterward. The thing about not smoking a cigarette is you miss everything about it.

I put the cigarette back on the card table and looked at my notes.

I knew how this trial would play out. If I sat on the jury, how would I vote?

How would the sitting jury vote if the trial were held today?

What did I know about Utah?

I knew that sixty percent of the people who lived there were Mormons. I knew the Catholic population was ten percent or less, which made the odds of Hughes winding up in a Catholic orphanage a ten to one shot. It became the forty-fifth state in January of 1896. It was named after the Ute Indian tribe. They had great skiing and a decent basketball team. Butch Cassidy was born there in 1866.

That's what I knew about Utah, which wasn't much.

It was getting late and I needed to make a decision.

Sweat helps me think.

A few months ago, I built a pull-up/chin-up bar, an elevated push-up station and purchased a heavy bag with a two hundred pound, water-filled base.

I stood up from the lawn chair and removed my shirt.

I went to the pull-up bar and did ten reps. Immediately, I lowered myself to the push-up station and did twenty-five of those. I repeated this procedure ten times until my chest ached, my shoulders burned and my arms gave out from exhaustion.

I rested for five minutes.

Then I slipped on bag gloves and hit the heavy bag one thousand times.

When I sat down in the lawn chair, I was as soaked as if I took a shower with my clothes on.

I made the decision.

I would go to Utah to tie up the loose ends.
I celebrated my decision by lighting the cigarette.
It tasted pretty damn good.

CHAPTER 11

I was walking out the door of my trailer a minute or so after eight the following morning when my hard line phone rang.

I answered it and Janet said, "My life was a great deal less complicated when you were off somewhere being a drunk and not in my life."

"So was mine," I said.

"I acted childish last night, didn't I?"

"I wrote the book on it," I said. "Stupid, too."

"Hey, whose apology is this?"

"Neither," I said. "We're still in the feeling-out process."

"Mark doesn't come home from school until 3:45," Janet said. "And I'm off today. Maybe I could give you a little something else to feel?"

"That is the best offer I've had all day."

"The day just started."

"And very well, I might add."

"So?"

"I can make it by two," I said. "I've got a date with the sheriff at ten. Want me to bring lunch?"

"I could imagine what you'll bring," Janet said. "Don't worry, I'll fix something edible. Don't be late. The early bird and all that."

I had just hung up and walked out the door when Lieutenant Walter Grimes, my ex-partner and closest friend, exited his unmarked sedan.

"You're out early," Walt said.

"Early has a way of turning late," I said.

"Where you off to?"

"Meet Sheriff Jane."

"I figured your hand was in the pie when I saw fancy-pants Clark on the news," Walt said. "Care for a ride-along?"

"I don't think Jane would mind, but it's a long way for something out of your jurisdiction," I said.

"I've known Simms as long as you have," Walt said. "We'll take my car."

"Can we hit Pat's on the way out?"

"You buying?"

"I don't remember you being this cheap when we were partners."

"We're still partners in spirit and I'm frugal."

"Frugal meaning penny-pinching."

"Hey, I didn't ask for gas money, did I?"

At Pat's, I picked up a box of six for later and two coffees for the road.

"So what does it look like?" Walt said as he drove and sipped.

"Like she's guilty as sin," I said.

"And what does it look like to you?"

"It looks like a lonely career woman picked up a young stud for a quick roll in the hay and killed him in a drunken rage of self-loathing," I said.

"Been spending a lot of time with that priest psychiatrist, I see."

"I get blessed and analyzed at the same time, plus I get to save my soul."

"You didn't answer my question," Walt said.

I pulled out my pack of smokes.

"Hey, don't even," Walt said as I lit one.

I blew a great, big smoke ring.

"This is a government car," Walt said.

"Quit whining," I said. "And to answer your question, what I think is where the evidence takes me." I blew another smoke ring. "Just like you."

"This car doesn't have an ashtray," Walt said.

"It doesn't need one," I said as I flicked ashes out the window.

Walt glared at me the remainder of the drive.

"Hi, Walt," Jane said when we arrived at the Peek A Boo Motel. "You're a bit out of your territory, aren't you?"

"It's a ride-along," I said. "Only I'm not sure who's the along."

Jane was standing against her cruiser with a container of coffee. We stopped at a convenience store a few blocks away from the motel for three fresh coffees, which I held in a paper bag in my left hand. Her eyes immediately went to the Pat's bag in my right hand.

"Bekker, you are aware of the ongoing cholesterol and obesity battle we have in this country?" Jane said.

"That's why we only get two apiece," I said. "You have the room key?"

Jane dangled the key. "Let's eat the donuts inside," she said. "It's bad for our image to be seen in public with powdered sugar on our chins."

"What image is that?" Walt said.

Room 15 had a queen-size bed, a small sofa against the wall with a coffee table in front of it, a television with cable, a dresser with a mirror, a phone and a bathroom. We sat on the sofa to drink our coffee and eat our donuts.

Nothing had been touched since the night of the incident.

The blood had dried black and thick on the rug.

The bed was unmade and stained black.

All clothing and personal items were in evidence at Jane's office.

"It's a lot of blood," Walt said as he bit into a lemon cream.

"The kid died hard," I said as I tackled a Boston cream. "He bled a great deal before he died."

"Which means what?" Jane said as she wiped cream from her lemon donut off her chin with a finger and then licked it clean.

We all sipped coffee.

"It could mean Simms stabbed him twice on the bed and he rolled off onto the rug," I said. "Explaining the thump the couple in the next room heard. He lay bleeding for a while, either passed out or too drunk to move. Simms falls off the bed on top of him, explaining the repeated thumps the couple next door heard, which prompted their 911 call."

Jane nodded as she nibbled on her donut. "It fits, doesn't it?"

"Warm in here," Walt said. "Not good for the evidence."

I looked at the wall where a circular thermostat was located. I stood up, walked to the wall, and inspected it. The dial controlled central air and heating. It was set at seventy-eight degrees.

"What was the weather that day?" I said.

"I don't even know what it is today," Walt said.

"Unusually cool for this time of year," Jane said. "Hold on a minute." She pulled out her iPad and pushed some buttons. "High sixty-two, low of forty-nine."

"So by the time they leave the bar, it's cold and they crank up the heat," I said.

"Unless you think she killed him because she was cold, so what?" Walt said.

I lowered the dial to sixty-eight and returned to the sofa.

"Speaking from . . ." I said.

The air conditioning came on with a soft hum. Above the bed, to the left and right, were air vents. The slatted kind so the warm or cold air blew downward onto the bed.

"Speaking from a great deal of experience, when you're drunk as a skunk, you really don't feel the cold all that much," I said. "Maybe if it was thirty-two degrees, but at around sixty, I wouldn't even notice."

"My wife's always cold," Walt said. "Always bitching about it, making me feel her nose like a puppy."

"Maybe she doesn't know how to dress?" Jane said.

"In the house with the heat on?" Walt said.

"So Simms is cold, is that a motive for murder?" Jane said.

"No," I said. "I'm just throwing stuff at the wall to see what sticks."

"I'll tell you what sticks," Walt said. "This goddamn donut, right in my throat."

"If you don't want your other one, I'll take it," Jane said.

"I didn't say that," Walt snapped.

"Jane, how long will this room be secured?" I said.

"Until prosecutor, defense and judge say otherwise."

I nodded.

"Let's take a ride to Simms's house and see if we can find the serial number of her .32," I said.

Carly Simms lived in a villa-style house about thirty minutes from the motel. It was large enough for two, but too small for a family. Two bedrooms, one large, the other not, kitchen, living room, dining area, laundry room, and a forty-foot fenced-in backyard. The front door was solid oak. The sliding doors in the kitchen led to the backyard.

Simms used the second bedroom as her study. There was a locking desk, a second desk for computer and printer, a locking four-tier file cabinet. Jane had the desk key and unlocked it. We found a photocopy of Simms's 4473, the government form required when you purchase a firearm. The serial number for the .32 was recorded on the form. I jotted down the number in my small notepad.

"I'll have it circulated to the pawn shops and gun stores," Jane said.

"Jane, how are her finances?" I said.

"Frozen until she posts bail."

"Will she?"

"It will be high. At least a hundred and fifty thousand."

"Clark will post," I said. "Then she can write me a check."

"For?"

"My plane ticket and expenses to Utah."

"Besides Mormons, what's in Utah?" Walt said.

"Orphanages and loose ends."

"Meaning?" Walt said.

"I'll tell you about it on the way back," I said. "Jane, who has better intel, you or Walt?"

"Are you kidding?" Jane said. "I run things on a county sheriff's budget."

"Then you won't mind if I use Walt for intel patched into you?"

"I have very little ego," Jane said. "About the size of my budget."

"I'll call Clark later and see what the status is on bail," I said.

"We're through here?" Jane said.

I nodded.

"Good," Jane said. "I have a nail appointment at noon."

CHAPTER 12

"The prosecution will go for the throat on this one," Walt said. "Like those spiders that eat their own, they want to make a point. Plus, she's hated on both sides."

I lowered my car window and lit a smoke.

"Clark is no lightweight," I said.

"This is different," Walt said. "Simms is a player on the team. The state will want to show the public that favors are not granted because one of their own fucked up. They'll make a point of it."

I glanced at Walt.

"They'll do whatever they can to discredit her in the media and on the witness stand," Walt said. "They'll do the promiscuous slut, man-eater routine 24-7 to discredit her to the jury and take anybody down in the process to win their case."

"What the fuck are you talking about?" I said.

"Me."

"What about you?"

"Christ, it was so long ago, I can't even remember," Walt said. "Before Carol, before you started drinking. We had an affair. It . . ."

"Stop," I said.

"Stop what?"

"The fucking car."

"We're on the highway."

"I don't care if we're on the fucking moon. Stop the god-damn car."

Walt slowed into the breakdown lane, stopped and put the car in park.

I got out, tossing the cigarette.

Walt got out.

I went around to his side and shoved him into the door.

"You stupid fuck," I said.

"It lasted only a week," Walt said.

I shoved him again, harder.

"Quit that," Walt said.

"How long you married, twenty-five years?"

"It was the only time I cheated on Elizabeth."

"And if it comes out now in open court, what happens?"

"I get divorced," Walt said. "And I don't want to get divorced."

I shoved Walt one more time for good measure.

"Stupid fuck," I said.

"Can we go now?" Walt said. "While my spine is still intact."

Back on the road, I lit another cigarette.

"So what happened?"

"Nothing," Walt said. "I was thirty-five and feeling sixty. She was younger and hot as a firecracker. You were off doing your RICO thing and we worked on a minor case together. Next thing you know, we're shacked up in a motel. I came to my senses after a few days and that was that. We both agreed it was stupid and never to speak of it."

"Elizabeth know?"

"Do you see the ring on my finger?" Walt said. "It wouldn't be there if she knew. Elizabeth is not what you would call a forgiving woman."

"Stupid," I said.

"Agreed," Walt said. "So what now? I've been thinking about

57

this since I saw the news. As much as I don't want to see her burn if she isn't guilty or walk if she is, I don't want to lose my wife in the process of finding out."

"I'll talk to Clark," I said. "Maybe the line of questioning doesn't have to go that way and past lovers and names don't need to be brought up."

Walt looked at me.

We both knew that it would.

A prosecutor hungry to burn someone will walk every avenue presented. They would paint Simms as a man-eating bitch to discredit her to the jury and names would go flying through the air like paper airplanes.

"Prosecution will discredit her any way possible," Walt said.

"I'll talk to Clark," I said.

CHAPTER 13

"I have to go to Utah for a few days," I said.

"What's in Utah?"

We were under the covers. I was covered in sweat. Janet was cool as a cucumber. I thought about feeling her nose, but resisted the temptation.

"Loose ends. Unanswered questions. Information I think I can obtain only by talking to people who knew the victim."

"When?"

"Day after tomorrow, if I can swing it."

"Is she guilty?"

"I think so, but the whole thing doesn't make sense," I said. "Murder, like all other crimes, just isn't that complicated. MOM usually covers all the bases and generally it's never wrong."

"MOM?"

"Method, opportunity, motive," I said. "Method, a letter opener to the heart. Opportunity, drunk in the motel room. Motive, unknown. Usually, your gut kicks in and if you think the husband did it, most times it turns out to be the husband."

"So motive is missing in your MOM thing?"

"That's kind of a big one."

"You think the motive is in Utah?"

"I don't know what I think," I said. "But loose ends dangling in the wind most times spells disaster for the defendant."

"She's really attractive, isn't she?" Janet said.

"We covered that one this morning," I said. "I thought I was off the hook."

"Hear me out," Janet said. "Here's a woman used to having men go Lady Gaga over her when she walks into a room."

"What's a Lady Gaga?"

"Oh, boy," Janet said. "Okay, put another way, she's used to men fawning and falling over her and maybe this guy, once they were in the room, didn't find her so attractive anymore. Her female ego is bruised. She's drunk. She grabs her letter opener and stabs him out of scorn."

"I thought of that," I said. "But, Hughes is twenty-three years old. Even if he doesn't find Simms as attractive as he thought, he's going to refuse a freebie from her once they're in the motel room? It doesn't quite add up from a twenty-three-year-old male point of view."

"What if he was too drunk to perform? She could interpret that as rejection given they were both gassed enough to pass out."

"That one I'll look into."

Janet glanced at her bedside alarm clock. "Feel like a bite of lunch?"

"Yeah. Question, though. I'm sweating and you're not. When do you feel cold?"

"Women run differently than men. Sixty-five degrees, I'm ready for a sweater."

"Say forty-nine or fifty?"

"The heat comes on. Why?"

"Just another one of those loose ends."

Janet tossed off the covers.

"Get dressed before you have to eat loose ends for lunch."

Chapter 14

I was grilling some hot dogs and burgers when Oz wandered over from his trailer. About five hundred feet separate us on the beach. Otherwise, we're alone most of the time, unless you count gulls squawking for handouts and dudes riding waves at high tide.

"Pick up the beans and cornbread from town?" Oz said as he slid into his chair next to mine.

"I did," I said. "Beans are keeping warm on the stove."

Around sixty-eight or -nine, Oz is a handsome black man who gave thirty-five years of his life to the postal service. He retired after a drunk behind the wheel of a pickup smashed into his car, killing his wife and daughter. His daughter's head was severed and wound up in his lap. He was already drinking heavily when I moved into my trailer and we went down that slippery slope of drinking heavily to alcoholism together. We've both been sober eight months now and have dinner on the beach several times a week when I'm not at Janet's.

I flipped the burgers, rolled the dogs, took a seat and lit a cigarette.

"Days are getting longer," Oz said. "But there's still a chill in the night air off the ocean."

"Want me to build a fire?"

"Be nice."

There's a wire trash basket beside the grill. I keep it filled with newspaper and wood for just such nights. I lit a wood match and set fire to the paper, then took my seat.

"I checked the schedule before I came over," Oz said. "There's a couple of good games on we can watch. That kid in San Francisco pitching, the Yankees at Boston."

I rolled out the television with a thirty-foot-long extension cord and we ate before a roaring fire in the basket and watched baseball. What's better than that for two old guys with nothing else to do?

By the seventh inning, I added wood to the fire as the temperature off the ocean was around fifty-five degrees.

"Good night to put the heat on before you go to bed," I said.

Oz nodded. "Never bothered me when I was drinking," he said. "This chilly air. But then again, I wouldn't remember if it did. Could be snowing on me so long as I had a bottle to keep me warm."

"Miss it?"

"The drinking? Only every waking moment. Not the hang-overs, though."

While they stretched after the seventh inning, I went inside for a pot of coffee and two mugs. I filled each mug and gave one to Oz.

"Here's to no hangover in the morning," I said.

"And a warm fire on a chilly night," Oz added.

The Frisco game went to the eleventh inning. Oz fell asleep after the ninth. I added more wood and let him sleep. I drank coffee, smoked, watched the game and thought about Simms.

One bad evening was all it took to end one life, send another to prison for life or the death penalty and possibly destroy a twenty-five-year marriage.

One bad evening.

It was too late to do anything besides go to bed. I woke Oz and waited until he made it home to his trailer, then I went inside and locked up.

Sleep was in short supply. My body was ready for sleep, but my mind wasn't.

I tossed and turned, avoided looking at the alarm clock and finally around three in the morning, gave up. I sat on the sofa with a glass of milk and a cigarette. If Molly were here, she would sit beside me and beg to be patted.

Molly wasn't here.

Something Janet said nagged at me.

If rejected, could Simms become so outraged that she would kill Hughes in a drunken rage?

Was she rejected?

Was Hughes too drunk to perform?

If push came to shove, would I defend a woman I believed guilty?

If push came to shove, would I allow a woman I believed to be innocent to destroy the marriage of my best friend if it helped prove her innocence?

I pretended the milk was a double shot of single-malt Scotch and downed it in one mighty gulp, then returned to bed and did battle with the covers.

Eventually the covers won.

CHAPTER 15

Clark, Simms and I sat at the conference table in Clark's office and watched cable news on a flat-screen television. It was HD and the colors were brilliant. I thought that maybe I should pick one up for watching baseball games with Oz. Probably see the seams of a fastball in 3D or 4-G, or whatever they were selling these days.

Adjectives such as "diva," "femme fatale" and "cougar" were tossed around to describe Simms by the smarmy reporters. They did everything short of describing her as a kitten killer to drive their talking points home.

The scene at the courthouse after Simms posted two hundred thousand in bail was a three-ring flea circus, with reporters pounding her and Clark as they made their way to a waiting limo.

Clark's only comment was to repeat, "No comment at this time," from the courthouse steps to the open limo door.

Simms had nothing to say. To her credit, she didn't try to hide her face. What was the point? There was hours of her on file footage. She wore a power suit with the skirt above the knee and black high heels. A reporter commented on the suit with, "She appears every inch the Cougar Killer," and it was picked up by others.

Cougar Killer became the mantra of the day.

"What's all this cougar business about?" Clark said as he used a remote to turn off the television.

"An unmarried woman of my age who preys on men half her age is called a cougar," Simms said.

"I know what it means," Clark said. "But these cable assholes are trying to paint you as some middle-aged, desperate bitch, preying on children, for God's sake."

"A 24-7 news cycle needs to be filled," Simms said. "And a female state prosecutor accused of murder, especially when it's a sexually charged, smoking gun–type of case, is O.J. material, as they suggested."

"How the fuck am I . . . ?" Clark said. "Never mind." He picked up the landline phone on the conference table and pushed a button. "Get the judge who issued bail on the Simms case on the phone," he barked when his receptionist picked up. "Tell him right now."

Clark hung up and looked at me.

"What's the terms of bail?" I said.

"House arrest, no passport, driver's license," Clark said. "She can leave the house only in the company of her attorney or someone I appoint as such."

"I'm going to Utah," I said. "Tomorrow morning."

Clark opened the file in front of him and removed a plain white envelope.

"Take it," Clark said. "For the trip."

I opened the envelope. It contained one thousand dollars in cash, another thousand in traveler's checks and a Visa card issued to the Lewis and Clark law firm in my name.

"I have to crack open my life's savings to pay Bekker for this," Simms said. "I'll probably go through my 401 as well before this is over."

"Think if you had to pay my bill," Clark said.

"I know that," Simms said. "And I'm grateful for your kindness."

"Don't worry about that now," Clark said. "Bekker had some . . ."

The phone rang. Clark scooped it up immediately.

"Your Honor, David Clark," he said. "I realize there is very little you can do to control the media, but how am I supposed to select twelve impartial jury members with this kind of slanderous news coverage? Cable news is convicting my client on television before indictment proceedings, for God's sake. Every jury member we interview will be thinking Cougar Killer before the trial even starts."

Clark held the phone to his ear as he listened to the judge.

"I'm afraid if this keeps up, I'll have to request a change of venue to try the case in Ohio," Clark said.

He listened to the judge again, this time a bit longer.

"Yes, Your Honor, I will," Clark said. "Thank you. Goodbye."

He hung up and looked at me. "Said a change of venue wasn't necessary at this time. I knew he'd say that, but I wanted to plant the seed for my anti-media campaign tirade."

"Do you think a mistrial is possible?" I said.

"Anything is possible," Clark said. "You said on the phone this morning that you had something you wanted to discuss."

I looked across the table at Simms.

"How would you feel about taking a polygraph?" I said.

"Pointless," Simms said. "I can't lie about something I can't remember and it won't be admissible in court. You know that."

"That doesn't matter," I said.

"I agree, take it," Clark said. "Bekker wants to play the media game and turn it against them. News of you passing a test does just as much persuading on a jury as does negative coverage. And besides, it's impossible to un-hear something once you've heard it no matter what a judge says."

Simms nodded her head. "I'll take it."

"The other thing is, I'd like to have you work with a hypnotist to try to regain some of your lost memory," I said. "It's possible to remember a great deal under hypnosis that you wouldn't normally."

"Bekker, I have to admit," Clark said. "You constantly surprise me. Do you know anybody who is qualified?"

"No."

"I do," Clark said.

"Get him," I said.

We both looked at Simms.

"Simms?" Clark said.

"I'm willing," Simms said. "I've never really believed in hypnosis before, but I'm willing to try just about anything at this point to prove my innocence."

"Good. I'll make the call and set it up," Clark said.

"One more thing and don't even think about lying," I said. "The prosecution, your former office, is going to paint you as the next Lizzie Borden and the media will run with that. You had an affair with Lieutenant Grimes and that won't look so good for both of you if it comes out. You need to make a list, check it twice and give it to Clark of anybody you slept with that could impact the trial."

"I forgot all about Walt," Simms said. "It was so long ago. He told you?"

"He doesn't want to lose his wife if it comes out in court. I don't blame him."

Simms nodded.

"Does anybody else know about that affair?" Clark said.

"Not to my knowledge," Simms said.

"Good," Clark said. "Let's make a list of anybody that might even suspect."

"I'll call you from Utah tomorrow," I said.

"Wait a minute, Bekker," Simms said. "I need to ask you something."

I looked at Simms.

"Do you think I killed that man?" Simms said.

"It doesn't matter what I think," I said.

"It does to me," Simms said.

"Point blank, I don't know," I said.

Simms nodded. "At least you're honest. Which is why I wanted you on my side."

"You may regret it before this is through," I said.

"An enemy stabs you in the back," Simms said. "A friend stabs you in the front. Are you my friend, Bekker?"

Driving home, I thought that whoever coined the phrase "Honesty is the best policy" never had his wife ask him if the new dress she just picked out made her look fat.

Or if someone was guilty of first-degree murder.

CHAPTER 16

I caught an early morning business flight to Salt Lake City, Utah, that set me down just after nine-thirty in the morning, adjusting for the two-hour time zone difference.

For the entire three-hour flight, something nagged at me. A detail, a word, a phrase, a look, something I couldn't put my finger on drilled a hole in the back of my skull and made a comfortable home for itself.

In the terminal, I retrieved my suitcase and went to the rental booth for the car I'd reserved on the phone. I'd requested a car with a GPS, but the one presented me didn't have one. I had a thirty-minute wait for one that did. I used the time to eat breakfast at a restaurant on the main floor of the terminal.

I thought about what nagged at me while I ate scrambled eggs with potatoes, bacon, toast and coffee. I wasn't firing on all cylinders. Maybe it was the early plane ride? Maybe it was the lack of anything in the way of evidence for and not against? Maybe it was that all my training was in arresting the guilty and not trying to prove them innocent?

Maybe it was because I had a client who was too drunk to remember if she committed murder or not?

Maybe I should go fetch the rental, drive to the orphanage and let the facts fall where they may? Maybe that was a good idea?

The rental was a mid-size sedan with GPS, CD player, satellite radio and some other stuff I would never use because I couldn't figure it out or had no use for it. I entered the address for the Sacred Heart Orphanage into the GPS and let it guide me thirty miles south of Provo to some beautiful countryside in the middle of nowhere.

Nowhere is an ideal location for a boys' orphanage. It's difficult to run away from, isolated from outside influences and provides plenty of fresh air and the opportunity for hard work in the outdoors.

Brother Philip Lewis Anderson was the man to see. He was the director of the orphanage. I didn't have an appointment. When I arrived at the gate, I told the security guard in the booth who I was and who I'd come to see. He made a call to the offices and I was allowed into the compound.

I drove from gate to main complex and parked in one of several dozen visitors' spots. Only a few other cars were in the lot. I guess it was a slow day for visitors at the orphanage.

Sacred Heart occupied four hundred acres of land nestled between some serious hills in the background. Sixty acres consisted of farmland where, at a glance, I could see corn stalks growing and what looked like rows of potatoes and lettuce.

The main complex consisted of grammar school, middle school and high school buildings, a large church, a gym facility, two barns—one for cattle, the other for horses—several tool sheds, a string of offices, a medical facility and a workshop.

Brother Philip met me at the stairs of the offices. He was a big man of about sixty, with thinning hair and wide, round glasses. He wore a lightweight suit and tie. There was nothing about his appearance that suggested he was a Catholic Brother. I don't know what I was expecting to find. Maybe a brown robe with a belt of rosary beads, sandals and a shaved bald spot on his head.

We shook hands. His grip was firm and dry.

"I have to say that when Sheriff Morgan called me with the

news about Jon Hughes, I was deeply saddened and taken aback," Brother Philip said. "I still am."

"What else did the sheriff tell you?" I said.

"She said you are a private detective gathering facts for the defense."

"I used to be a cop, a detective with Special Crimes," I said. "I'm retired from the job and do this now."

Brother Philip nodded. "Where would you like to talk?"

"It's a beautiful day," I said. "Why don't you give me a tour while we talk?"

"We have one hundred and sixty-eight boys between the ages of five and eighteen," Brother Philip said as we walked to the edge of the farmland. "All the fruits and vegetables we eat are grown right here by our boys. All desserts are baked using what we grow, also by our boys, taught and supervised by our live-in chef. We have one hundred chickens for eggs. The boys feed and tend to them daily. There are eight milk cows, cared for by the boys. Our entire dairy is made here, even the butter. We have eight riding horses and those who wish to learn to ride must also learn to care for them. We have a full athletic program, including gymnastics and swimming. And of course, our primary goal is education."

"And how do the boys happen to arrive here?" I said.

"We're a Catholic facility," Brother Philip said. "Women who do not wish to have abortions have the option of giving birth and delivering the child to us for the purpose of adoption. We also take children whose parents have been killed and there are no family members to raise them. Sometimes, children are taken from parents by the courts and we raise them. They can and do come from all parts of the country and from many different circumstances."

"All faiths?"

"We don't use faith as a guiding tool," Brother Philip said.

"Ten percent of our boys at present are Mormons. We also have Jewish boys and Protestant boys. All faiths are welcome here."

We wandered over to the barns where some older boys were grooming horses.

"Tell me about Jon Hughes," I said.

"He was with us . . ." Brother Philip said and paused when his voice cracked.

I waited.

Brother Philip regrouped.

"Jon came to us at the age of seven when his parents died in a car accident," Brother Philip said. "What little family he had were in no position to raise him. They offered him to us and he stayed with us until he left for college at the age of eighteen."

"What kind of a kid was he?"

"High spirited, a lot of trouble at times, very bright and a great student," Brother Philip said.

"Let's take it one at a time," I said. "High spirited means?"

"He was very outgoing," Brother Philip said. "He made friends easily, loved to ride horses, was a great athlete, learned boxing and karate. He had a very competitive nature. He hated to lose, but wasn't a sore loser when he did."

"Trouble at times means?"

"There was a great deal of anger in him, especially the first few years. Not just from losing his parents, but at having family that didn't want him. He got into many fights with other boys until he entered the boxing and martial arts program where he had an avenue for that anger."

"Bright and a good student?"

"Bright as in his senior-year IQ maxed out at 143," Brother Philip said. "A good student in that his grades were never less than A minus. As a senior, he took computer science courses and excelled. It came as no surprise he went to college to study that and later found employment with a computer company as a designer."

"Did he keep in touch with you after he left?" I said.

"Yes. He visited several times a year and often made cash donations once he started making a decent salary."

"As a man, did he ever talk to you about women, a girlfriend, anything?"

"Not really," Brother Philip said. "I had the feeling he was too busy building a career to think about settling down. He was only approaching twenty-four. There would have been plenty of time for a wife and family."

Would have been, I thought.

"What about friends?"

"He had many here that he kept in touch with afterward."

"And you know that how?"

"From his visits. He would give me updates on some of them."

"Can you give me a list of his friends?" I said.

"Would you stay for lunch?" Brother Philip said. "That would give me time to think and prepare a list."

"Sure."

Lunch was pasta made from wheat grown on the farm with sauce made from tomatoes and spices grown next to the wheat, garlic bread baked fresh, cold milk or lemonade and fresh apple pie for dessert made from a small orchard behind a barn.

The older boys prepared the meal and served it. The younger boys ate.

I sat with Brother Philip at the table reserved for his staff. Thirty Brothers in all, two nuns who were nurses and six laymen who also were teachers.

After introductions, Brother Philip and I talked freely as if no one else heard our conversation.

"I've been thinking about Jon's friends, here and when he left us," Brother Philip said. "I can name six with certainty, but I don't have recent contact information on them. It has been almost six years, after all."

"Names will do fine," I said.

"We'll go to my office after dessert."

The one hundred and sixty-eight boys and young men watched me with keen interest. They knew I wasn't a visitor for one of them and I didn't look like a Brother or a member of the church.

Therefore, they reasoned someone was in trouble.

They reasoned correctly.

It just wasn't one of them.

Brother Philip's office wasn't small, but appeared so due to clutter. File cabinets, stacks of files, boxes of files, the entire office was a fire code violation.

I moved a file box off a chair opposite the desk and sat in it to wait for Brother Philip to hand-write his list. After several minutes of thinking and writing, he handed it to me.

"It's the best I can do for now," Brother Philip said. "If you leave me a phone number, I'll call you with more if I remember."

"Sure."

I folded the list into a pocket without looking at it, shook Brother Philip's hand for the second time today, returned to my rental and drove an hour north to the TRAX Corporation.

CHAPTER 17

The TRAX Corporation building, a four-story structure that appeared constructed entirely of glass, sat nestled against a lush landscape in the country. There wasn't another building for a half mile in either direction. The parking lot held two hundred cars. I knew because there were five rows deep of twenty across. It was less than half-full. Maybe I came at a bad time, or maybe they worked in shifts.

I parked in the third row, shielded my eyes from the afternoon sun glaring off the building, and entered the expansive, ultra-modern lobby. A security guard sat behind a visitor's desk off to my left.

I showed my identification to the guard and requested to speak with Jon Hughes's manager. The news must have reached the guard because he showed me his eyes and they weren't pleased.

"Who you working for?" the guard said.

His voice was full of sudden hostility.

"Unless you were Hughes's supervisor, that's none of your business," I said.

"Jon was a friend of mine," the guard said. "We were in the home together. He got me this job. I think that makes it my business."

I took a closer look at the guard. He was a kid all of twenty-two, or -three.

"I think you're right," I said. "How about we talk after I see his boss? I'd like to hear what you have to say."

"My name is Josh. I'll call up to Sal. He was Jon's boss."

"Okay, Josh. Thanks. Is it okay to smoke outside?"

"They have a designated area to the left. You'll see one of those stand-up ashtrays."

I went outside and found one of those long-necked plastic ashtrays against the wall. I lit a cigarette and by the time it was done, Sal was coming off the elevator.

Sal was Sal Meeks, division manager for TRAX Corporation and a games designer. He was about forty and casually dressed in chinos and a polo shirt with loafers on his feet. What was left of his hair was worn in a ponytail. It reminded me of Hulk Hogan, the wrestler. Someone once said of Hogan that for a bald guy he sure has a lot of hair.

I could say the same of Sal Meeks.

"Mr. Bekker, is that right?" Sal said when I met him at the desk.

"Yes."

"Josh said you're a private detective. Can I see some ID?"

I flashed my license.

Sal nodded. "Please understand that Jon . . . that this is a big shock to us."

"I understand. Is there someplace we can talk?"

"My office or the coffee bar?"

"Let's start at the coffee bar," I said. "My treat. I'm on an expense account."

On the second floor, the coffee bar resembled the kind you find in large bookstores where the brainy types sip, read and never actually buy a book. It overlooked the gardens behind the building where a large lily pond dominated the scenery.

I got two coffees and we sat at a window table, but then again, the entire building was one giant window. A dozen or so employees were sprinkled among the thirty or so tables. I spotted more than one ponytailed male sipping coffee. They paid us no mind. I had the feeling TRAX Corporation was a very casual company to work for.

"All I'm trying to do is tie up some loose ends and fill in some blanks for the defense lawyer," I began. "Nothing said here has anything to do with the defendant's guilt or innocence."

"Innocence?" Sal said. "My understanding is they caught her with a smoking gun in the room with Jon. Don't tell me they actually think she might be innocent?"

"I didn't say that," I said. "That's for a jury to decide, not me or you. Whatever information I gain here is shared equally by defense and prosecutor through Motion of Discovery. That's the law."

"What kind of loose ends?" Sal said.

I removed a small notebook and a pen from my inside jacket pocket. "Background info on Mr. Hughes, mostly."

"I'll agree only if you allow me to make copies of your notes," Sal said.

"Sure."

"What kind of loose ends?"

We talked for about an hour.

I learned that Hughes started working for TRAX Corporation as a junior graphics designer and worked his way up to design engineer inside of eighteen months because he was just so damn talented. So said Sal Meeks.

Hughes worked on six major video games for some of the biggest game companies in the world. His services were so sought after, clients actually put in bids for his work. "In another two years, Jon could have gone out on his own and made millions for his work, he was that good," Sal said.

"Girlfriends?" I said.

"I'm sure he had some," Sal said. "He was a good-looking kid, but I think work was his priority at the moment."

"Did he talk about his childhood much?" I said. "The orphanage."

"No," Sal said. "We all knew about it, of course, but Jon never seemed to discuss it much, so we left it alone."

"The man he was supposed to meet, Harold Mitchell, do you know him?"

"Yes. His company is producing a new 3D game based on a slasher movie that was popular a few months ago. We sent a replacement to meet with him after . . . well, after."

I pulled out the list from Brother Philip and gave it to Sal.

"The director of the orphanage remembers these names as being close friends of Jon's from the time they lived there together," I said. "Do you recognize any of them?"

"One, yes," Sal said as he read the names. "The other five, no."

"Which one?"

"Josh Andrus," Sal said. "He works as a security guard for us."

"The kid downstairs?"

Sal nodded.

"Can I speak with him in private?" I said. "Maybe up here?"

"I'll send him on a thirty-minute break," Sal said. "Just remember to see me when you're done so I can copy your notes."

Somebody somewhere had stabbed Sal Meeks in the back. It was the only way to explain his paranoia about my notes.

"Sure."

CHAPTER 18

Josh Andrus removed his security guard jacket before he sat down opposite me at the table in the coffee bar. Up close, he was a big kid with a smooth baby face that didn't fit his large, athletic body.

"I'm glad we can talk, Josh," I said.

"Sure," Josh said.

"What I'm interested in is your friendship with Jon," I said.

"He was my friend," Josh said. "I loved him as if he were my real brother. Guys get close when you're in . . . a place like that."

I saw a fine mist form in Josh's soft brown eyes.

"How long were you in the home with Jon?" I said.

"Age of eleven to eighteen. That was five years ago I left."

"And you stayed friends afterward?"

"When you're that close, you don't stop being friends just because you left the home," Josh said.

I picked up my coffee and took a sip. "Would you like some coffee?"

"That would be good."

"My treat."

I went to the bar and returned with a coffee for Josh. He took a sip and I noticed the swelling on his knuckles.

"What happened there?" I said. "Your knuckles."

"That. Oh. Nothing happened. I study karate. Jon and me took lessons for ten years. It's what happens. Your knuckles and hands get hard."

"You must be pretty good by now."

"Third-degree black, same as Jon."

"I'm just curious as to how you arrived at Sacred Heart," I said.

"My mother gave me up at birth," Josh said. "I was in and out of orphanages for a long time, they tell me. I was in foster homes for a while, then sent to Sacred Heart by the state. I guess no one wanted me, same as Jon. Maybe that's another reason we were close."

"So you don't know who your mother and father are?" I said.

"No, do you?"

I looked at Josh.

"That was a joke," Josh said.

"And a good one," I said. "You had me there for minute. So tell me about Jon."

Josh spoke for about fifteen minutes. They were close buddies, as he put it, because when you have no family you make your own. After he left Sacred Heart, Josh bounced around for a while, working odd jobs and living wherever he could afford. Jon went to college, but Josh didn't have the smarts, so he did construction in the summer, moved snow in winter and lived at a boarding house in Salt Lake City. Jon got him the security guard job two years ago. It paid decent, had health benefits and was indoors out of the summer heat and winter cold. Jon had a few girlfriends, but nothing serious. He was too busy getting rich for serious relationships. In a couple of years, Jon planned to buy a big house and they would be roommates, along with some others from Sacred Heart. An orphanage without gates, Jon said.

"What about drinking or drugs?" I said.

"Jon never used drugs and only drank wine as far as I knew and he wasn't good at it," Josh said.

"Not good at it how?"

"He couldn't hold it," Josh said. "Some guys you'd never know they were drunk. With Jon, you knew. Two glasses and he was looped."

"Did you two still train together?" I said.

"Three times a week over at Tilton's Karate School in Provo."

"I think I have enough background information, Josh," I said. "Thank you."

"This woman, she's going to pay for what she did, right?"

"If the jury finds her guilty, she'll get life or maybe the death penalty," I said.

"Good."

"One last thing," I said and showed Josh my list of names. "Do you know any of these names?"

"Sure. They were in the home with us," Josh said. "I don't know where they are right now, but they were there with us back then."

"Brother Philip said Jon kept in touch with them."

"Yeah, that's like him," Josh said. "He liked to keep in touch with the guys. He probably has their addresses and phone numbers in his apartment in a book somewhere."

"If I need something else, can I call you?"

"Sure."

I shook Josh's hand.

I had the feeling he could crack walnuts in his grip.

CHAPTER 19

I loaded Jon Hughes's address into the GPS and it guided me a half hour east of the TRAX Corporation to an apartment complex in the sticks. Maybe twenty, four-story brown buildings made up the complex. Each apartment had a balcony off the kitchen. There was a pool and tennis courts. It was gated with a security guard at the entrance. It was the kind of cookie-cutter complex found from east to west coast, designed and occupied by the lower middle class.

I turned around and drove to the county sheriff's department not far away, parked and entered the Public Safety Building.

A deputy at the desk gave me a quick onceover. "Can I help you with anything?"

I showed my ID. "I'd like a few minutes of the sheriff's time," I said. "Concerning the murder of Jon Hughes."

"The kid who got stabbed back east?"

I nodded. "I'm gathering information for the attorney for the defense."

The sheriff's name was Millwood and he came downstairs from the second floor after the deputy made a quick call to his office.

"I'm Sheriff Millwood," he said.

"John Bekker. I work for the defense counsel, defending Carly Simms," I said. "I have a loose end you can help me with. It won't take long if you can spare some time."

"What loose end?"

82

I showed Millwood the list of names.

"Just doing some background info on Hughes," I said. "One of them works at TRAX, the other five I don't know. Hughes probably has their addresses and phone numbers in his apartment. I would like to talk with them before I fly home."

Millwood looked at his deputy.

"I'll be on cell phone," Millwood said.

We took Millwood's cruiser.

"You could do a name check with one phone call or a few clicks on a computer," Millwood said.

"I didn't have these names until a few hours ago," I said. "And a data bank check doesn't tell me if Hughes kept up with them or not."

Millwood nodded.

"I assume his rent is paid until the end of the month," I said. "What happens to his belongings after that?"

"They go to the county evidence storage facility if no one claims them," Millwood said.

"Anything of value, why not donate to Sacred Heart?" I said. "I'm sure they could use whatever you gave them."

"I'd have to see a judge to obtain permission, but that's not a bad idea," Millwood said.

We reached the gate and the guard on duty waved us in. Millwood drove to the complex manager's office in the first building. "I'll get the manager to let us in."

Jon Hughes had a one-bedroom apartment on the third floor, facing the backyard woods. There was a decent-size living room, a tiny kitchen, a small laundry room off the bathroom and the balcony.

The place was neat as a pin.

"No desk, no computer," Millwood commented as we toured the three rooms.

"Look for a date book, letters, anything like that," I said.

After an hour, we found nothing to indicate John Hughes kept in contact with the remaining five names given to me by Brother Philip.

I double-checked the walk-in closet, searching each pocket of all pants and jackets. Hanging neatly with his clothing were three sets of karate gear with black belts. That was about it, there was nothing else.

"Looks like that Brother was wrong about his friends," Millwood said.

"Looks like," I agreed. "Odd, though, that a young man who makes his living on a computer doesn't have one at home."

"Probably had a laptop like all the kids do these days," Millwood said. "Saves space in a small apartment like this."

"They didn't recover one in his room or his rental," I said.

I looked at the flat screen, 42-inch television in the living room. There was a full cable box on a shelf below the television. I fiddled with it for a moment.

"Wired for remote Internet access," I said.

"Does his laptop have anything to do with his murder?" Millwood said. "Or is it just a loose end for you guys?"

"Loose end," I said. "I didn't know he had one for sure until just now, but it makes sense."

"Look, Mr. Bekker, I'm just a small county sheriff, but all the loose ends in the world won't save that woman from a murder charge," Millwood said. "Even I can see that from half a country away."

"If you were conducting the investigation, would you want to talk with his friends and fill in the missing details, or would you just blow it off and walk away?" I said.

"I'd be doing the exact same thing you are," Millwood said. "What I can do is check with the cable provider. They might have a record of his laptop. I can check to see if it's turned up at any pawn shops anywhere."

"You'll let me know?"

"Sure."

"I'll be around until tomorrow afternoon," I said.

"I should have something by then," Millwood said.

He returned the key to the manager and by the time I retrieved my rental, it was after five. "I'm staying at the Comfort Inn by the airport," I said. "You can reach me there."

Millwood nodded and entered the Public Safety Building.

I took a shot and drove back to the TRAX Corporation. Josh Andrus got off duty at four and was long gone. The guard in his place said it was karate night.

I sat in the rental, smoked a cigarette and thought for a while.

Then I punched Tilton's Karate School into the GPS and followed the directions.

CHAPTER 20

Tilton's Karate School was a converted auto body shop located in downtown Provo. It was maybe five thousand square feet of open space. A class was in session when I found an empty space in the crowded parking lot.

I peeked in through the large window. About fifty students were going through warm-up exercises on a hardwood floor. It wasn't difficult to pick out Josh. A tall, muscular black man put them through their paces. There was an office. I opened the door and went in. Forceful shouts from the students as they went through their paces came through the door loud and clear.

The office walls were decorated with citations, degrees, photographs of the black man in various countries at other karate schools and tournaments. The wall behind a cluttered desk was reserved for his military history. Twenty years' worth of Army history, to be exact. A drill sergeant for the last ten of those twenty years, Tilton taught hand-to-hand combat to Army recruits and Rangers.

The office door opened and Tilton stepped inside. The shouts from the students were close to deafening. He closed the door and looked at me.

"Can I help you?" Tilton said.

I had my ID out and ready.

"I've been hired by the law firm defending the accused in the Jon Hughes case," I said. "Earlier, I spoke with Josh Andrus while he was at work. I have an additional question I need to ask him that might be important."

Tilton nodded. "There's forty-five minutes left in the session, can it wait?" he said. "I don't like to break my students' concentration."

"Sure."

"You're welcome to observe if you like."

I followed Tilton into the dojo and stood quietly in the corner while he put the students through their paces. Josh, by far the most advanced in the group, was singled out by Tilton for demonstrations to the others.

The session ended with nods and bows. Tilton told them to practice and stretch and be ready for the next session. There would be tests for yellow and brown belts.

Tilton escorted Josh toward me and we entered the office.

"Very impressive, Josh," I said. "It was a pleasure watching you train."

Josh beamed at me. "Thank you, Mr. Bekker."

"Josh and Jon Hughes were by far the most talented students I've ever trained," Tilton said.

"It shows," I said. "So, Josh, I have a quick question for you. Did Jon have a laptop computer?"

"Sure, man, the best," Josh said. "His job depended on that. It went everywhere he did. Even here when we trained."

"The police haven't recovered it as yet," I said. "Do you know what kind he had, what color, size, anything like that?"

"Sure," Josh said. "I saw it all the time. Must've weighed twenty pounds. Full screen, big carrying case, a lot of plug-ins. It was teal or maybe a bit lighter."

"Thanks, Josh," I said.

"Umm, Mr. Bekker?" Josh said. "I was wondering if you could give me a ride home. My car wouldn't start after work. I took two buses to get here."

"No problem," I said. "And thank you, Mr. Tilton. It was a pleasure."

"Give me a minute to change," Josh said, and left the office.

"Sure."

Tilton sat behind his desk and looked at me.

"Jon was growing into a fine man. Just make sure that woman gets what's coming to her," he said.

CHAPTER 21

"What's wrong with your car?" I said as I exited the parking lot at Tilton's.

"Besides being seventeen years old?" Josh said. "With two hundred and eighty seven thousand miles on it."

"Nuff said."

"You shouldn't smoke," Josh said.

"I'm not smoking."

"I can smell it in here. It gets in the upholstery."

"I was smoking," I said. "I'm not smoking now."

Josh cracked a grin at me.

"So Jon's laptop, how valuable do you think it is?" I said.

"Custom-made job like that, around ten thousand, I would guess. Maybe more."

"That much?"

"At least," Josh said. "It was pretty hi-tech for his job and all. I saw him sometimes designing games and things on it. He was a real whiz at stuff like that."

"Valuable enough to steal?"

"I guess. Why, you think it was stolen?"

"I don't know. It's definitely missing. Theft isn't out of the question."

"Maybe that woman took it before she killed him?"

"It wasn't in the room or his rental car," I said. "She was found passed out, so that's highly unlikely."

"I guess."

"Josh, did Jon have any enemies?" I said.

Josh turned in the seat to look at me. "Not that I know of," he said. "He wasn't that type of guy."

"What type is that?"

"You said I was impressive," Josh said. "You never saw Jon. He could take two of me, no sweat. Outside the dojo, he'd walk away from a fight every time. We celebrated his birthday last year at this sports bar in Salt Lake. Some drunks picked a fight. Jon could've wiped the floor with all of them, but he backed down and let them have their laugh at his expense. That type of guy."

"That's what Tilton teaches, isn't it? That fighting is a last resort?"

"Yeah, but Jon was that way, anyway."

"Hey, you know what?" I said. "I'm kind of hungry. Feel like a bite to eat before I drop you off?"

"That's a good idea," Josh said. "Nothing expensive. I'm kind of on a budget."

"I'm not," I said. "And it's my treat."

Josh grinned. "Oh, well, there is this place not far from here."

This place turned out to be an upscale sports bar with thirteen-dollar burgers, seven-dollar-a-plate fries and eight-dollar milkshakes.

Josh had two of each. I settled for single helpings. We both had the rice pudding with whipped cream for dessert, along with some really good coffee.

"That's another thing about Jon," Josh said as we ate our rice pudding. "He made like five or six times what I make and would've been a millionaire by the time he was thirty and never threw it in your face. You saw his apartment?"

"Yes."

"He could have lived way better than that," Josh said. "But he wasn't interested. He was saving his money to start his own company. We talked about it, how I could come work for him in a few years. He said it would be rough for a while, which is why he was saving everything he made."

We left it at that.

I drove Josh home.

He lived in one room in a boarding house that had seen better days.

I drove to my motel, took a hot shower before I settled in, and gave Janet a quick call at the hospital.

"I hate to stroke the male ego, but I miss you," Janet said. "When are you coming home?"

"I'm on a five p.m. flight tomorrow," I said.

"Have you learned anything?"

"I learned that I have more questions than answers," I said. "And that all things considered, I'd rather be there with you than here without you."

"Mark is going to his father's tomorrow afternoon," Janet said. "When you land, do not pass go, do not collect two hundred dollars. Just drive straight here with the idea in mind that you will be ravaged."

"I can do that," I said.

"Good," Janet said. "Night, sweetie. Duty calls."

I hung up and fell asleep watching an old Robert Mitchum movie where he was hunting a killer mountain lion in the old west. I'd seen it before. The mountain lion won.

CHAPTER 22

"I didn't expect to see you again so soon," Sal Meeks said as he met me in the lobby of the TRAX Corporation building. Josh wasn't behind the security desk, but an older man who seemed less than impressed with my presence.

"Or ever," I added.

"What can I do for you?" Sal said curtly. "I have several meetings to attend this morning."

"We've been unable to locate Jon's laptop," I said.

"A simple IP check can help you locate it if someone stole it and is using it online," Sal said.

"What's an IP?"

"Every computer has a built-in address that can be traced online when the user is searching the Web," Sal said. "That's how they look for child-porn users and for fraud. The cable company can probably get it for you."

"I spoke with Josh and he seemed to think it was a custom-made job."

"That's correct," Sal said. "Jon needed and depended on a computer that could do the things he needed. He had it made by a specialist in Provo. I've had work done there myself."

"Do you have a name and address?"

"Yes. I'll get it for you."

"By the way, I noticed Josh isn't at the desk."

"Rotating shifts. He comes on at four."

"I'll be gone by then. Tell him goodbye for me."

Sal nodded. "I'll be right back with that address."

Sheriff Millwood was at the State Police firing range when I arrived at the Public Safety Building. It wasn't far and I drove there hoping to catch him before he left. I just made it. He was walking to his cruiser when I pulled up beside him, parked and got out.

"Morning, Sheriff," I said. "They told me you would be here."

"I didn't get a rundown on the laptop, if that's what you're looking for," Millwood said.

"Actually, I have some new information," I said. "Ever hear of the PC Guru?"

We took Millwood's cruiser.

Able Billings was the PC Guru. About sixty, overweight, a long white beard, his graying hair in a ponytail, Billings more resembled an aging hippie Santa than a computer specialist.

Millwood told him the nature of our visit.

"Jon Hughes was a very good customer," Billings said. "I was sorry to hear what happened to him on the news."

"His laptop is missing," I said. "I understand it can be traced."

"If whoever stole it is stupid enough to use it without the capability of changing the IP address, it can," Billings said. "Give me a minute to check my files. Be right back."

Billings went into an office behind the counter. He was gone for several minutes. I took the time to shop around. I was more than impressed with the prices of his custom-designed laptops and home computers. So was Millwood.

"Eight grand for that?" Millwood said when he checked the price on a used laptop.

Billings returned. He had a slip of paper in his hand that he gave to me.

"Jon's laptop was some of my finest work," Billings said. "He was a good kid. Too young to go out that way."

"Or any way. Thanks," I said as I pocketed the slip of paper.

"I'll drop you at your rental," Millwood said when we returned to his cruiser. "Do me a favor and keep me up to date on this."

"Sure," I said.

CHAPTER 23

I rang Janet's doorbell prepared for a big sloppy with visions of us ripping our clothes off as we groped our way to the bedroom like a pair of teenagers on prom night.

Instead, I got a nun.

Sister Mary Martin, to be exact. She instantly read the concern on my face and took my left elbow to guide me inside the house.

"Regan is just fine, Mr. Bekker," Sister Mary Martin said to ease my concern. "It appears Mark's father has come down with the flu and Mark stayed home for the weekend. Janet thought it would make a nice surprise for you if Regan came to dinner."

"Sister, you just about gave me a heart attack," I said.

"You look fine to me," Sister Mary Martin said. "Regan and Mark are playing Frisbee in the backyard. Janet and I are in the kitchen. And . . ."

Molly came out from behind Sister Mary Martin and rubbed my ankles.

"I see her," I said and picked up the cat. "How are you, girl?"

I carried Molly into the kitchen.

Sister Mary Martin followed us.

Janet was stirring something on the stove. She gave me her smile, the one that said, oh well, the best-laid plans of mice and men aren't getting any nookie.

Sister Mary Martin opened the sliding doors and stepped out

to the yard.

I kissed Janet behind the neck.

"Disappointed?" Janet said.

"Never," I said. "I'll just have to redirect my energy into something else is all."

"Good," Janet said and gave me the wooden spoon. "Redirect it and stir this."

"What is it?"

"It will be chocolate pudding if you don't screw it up. Stir."

I stirred.

Janet went to the oven to remove a turkey. She set it on the counter to cool.

"You can make the whipped cream later," she said.

"I can?"

"Stir."

I stirred.

Janet started putting things on the table.

After a minute or so, the pudding started to bubble over. "Hey, something's happening here," I said.

"It's done," Janet said. "Remove it."

I put the pan on a back burner.

"Well, that's that," I said. "I'm exhausted."

"Not so fast, big boy," Janet said. "Help me set the table, then go get the kids."

I kissed Janet on the neck instead.

Sister Mary Martin came through the kitchen door from the yard. "Why don't you two get a room?" she said.

Regan and Mark came in behind Sister Mary Martin.

"Hey, Uncle Jack," Mark said.

Regan looked at me for a moment. Her eyes were wide and full of expression. She took a step, paused, then charged me and wrapped her arms around me in a tight hug.

I looked at Janet. She shrugged.

"What's all this then?" I said as I ran my hand over Regan's hair.

"You have a lot to be thankful for, Mr. Bekker," Sister Mary Martin said. "We'll talk about it over dinner."

Father Tomas began discussing Regan's leaving the hospital and living with me, the nun explained, and the hug I received was my daughter's way of telling me she approved of the plan.

"He feels that with Regan's commitment to learning new but basic things, she could be ready in as little as three months," Sister Mary Martin said.

"What things?" I said.

"Things that every young woman should know," Sister Mary Martin said. "Such as how to do laundry and prepare a simple meal. She understands that as fun as it might be, there comes a time when you have to put the crayons away if you're to grow up and become an accomplished woman."

I looked at Regan.

She nodded at me.

I looked at Sister Mary Martin.

"What about you?" I said.

"If you can stand my company five days a week, I'll be your housekeeper, so to speak," Sister Mary Martin said.

I looked at Regan.

She nodded at me.

"I guess I'll have to find a new place to live," I said. "One with a bit more room and fitting for a young woman."

Janet nodded at me.

After dinner and the dishes, Regan, Mark and Sister Mary Martin watched television for a bit while Janet and I took coffee in the backyard.

"I just want to throw something out there for you to think about," Janet said. "If we got married, you wouldn't need to find a new house for Regan. This one's ready made and plenty big enough for all of us."

I opened my mouth and Janet closed it with a look.

"Don't say anything. Not yet," she said. "I want you to say yes because you love me and because you want to, not because it's an easy way for Regan. Think about it. Just don't take forever. Forty-seven is no child bride, but I've still got a few good years left in me and I don't want to waste those chasing rainbows in the sky I can't catch."

"Hey, Mom?" Mark called from the kitchen door. "How about that chocolate pudding?"

"Just as soon as Uncle Jack makes the whipped cream," Janet said.

Chapter 24

The early morning sun was quickly warming the sand at my feet as I sipped coffee and set fire to a cigarette. I called Jane while I sipped and smoked.

"Learn anything from your trip?" Jane said.

"Oh, yeah," I said. "I learned that a whole lot of people thought Jon Hughes was the cat's meow. I learned that he was very good at his job and would have been a millionaire by age thirty. That a Catholic orphanage can thrive in the heart of Mormon country. That Hughes was highly skilled in karate and kept in regular touch with the orphanage and the guys he grew up with."

"Learn anything useful?" Jane said.

"Hughes had an expensive laptop filled with all kinds of design goodies that's gone missing," I said.

"Oooh," Jane said. "Now that's interesting."

"Yeah, but is it useful," I said. "Can you do something for me?"

"What?"

"I have a PI or IP or whatever the hell they call it number for his laptop," I said. "Maybe you can run it down along with some names."

"Names of?"

"Friends Hughes grew up with in the home," I said. "The director said Hughes kept in touch with them on a regular basis, but I can't find anything on them. There's one kid he spent time with, a Josh Andrus, I'll include his name with the others."

"And where will you be this fine day?" Jane said.

"Clark's office," I said. "Simms is having a polygraph test at ten."

"You the witness to the test?"

"A witness," I said. "Clark has someone from the prosecutor's office as the official witness."

"Even though it can't be used."

"Can't be used in court," I said. "A clean test result can be leaked to the media and that clouds a jury and adds some doubt no matter what anybody says."

"Call me when you're done raking Simms over the coals," Jane said. "I might have something for you by then."

I had seconds on the coffee and smokes before I showered and put on my best suit. It was my best suit because it was my only suit, so it won that distinction by default.

I reached Clark's office with fifteen minutes to spare. The polygraph examiner set up in the conference room. Simms, dressed casually in fashionable slacks and a button-down white shirt with pearl buttons, was already at the table when Clark escorted me in, along with the witness from the prosecutor.

The witness and I sat in chairs behind Simms so as not to create nervous tension on her part. The out of sight, out of mind thing.

The examiner began with the usual line of questions to establish a pattern of breathing, pulse rate and blood pressure variations for Simms under pressure. Once the actual test began, it took the better part of an hour. The questions were targeted to Simms's involvement in the murder of Jon Hughes on the night in question.

Thirty questions in all.

Twenty-eight times Simms answered, "I can't remember."

Two questions came from me during a ten-minute bathroom break.

Did you see a laptop computer belonging to Jon Hughes at any time during the evening in question?

Did Jon Hughes talk about his job, his friends or his upbringing?

No, was her answer to the first question.

Yes, to the part of the second question concerning Hughes's job. No to the other two parts pertaining to his friends or upbringing.

Simms, Clark, the witness and I filed into Clark's office to await the results of the test. It took about fifteen minutes for the examiner to come to his findings and enter the office.

"My expert opinion is that the subject Carly Simms is being totally truthful in her answers as recorded during the interview," he said. "I'll have results of the test sent to the prosecutor and defense for their records."

The witness glared at Simms.

"Just because she honestly doesn't remember doesn't mean she isn't guilty," he said and stormed out of the office.

"I'll send you my bill," the examiner said and followed the witness.

"He's right," Simms said. "That I was honest about not remembering doesn't mean I'm innocent. They'll paint it that way. I know. I helped train most of them. They're like sharks in a pool of blood when it comes to a conviction."

"They can paint whatever they want, but it helps me get a change of venue," Clark said. "Especially when the results of the test are leaked and they start crying foul and making a big deal about innocent of lying isn't innocent of murder and all that other crap. The more they whine, the better it is for us."

"Who is going to leak it?" I said.

"Don't worry about that," Clark said. "Carly, I've lined up a hypnotist, a highly skilled psychiatrist used by the courts all over the country. I'd like your permission to have him work with you and see if some sessions can jog a memory."

"I'd almost rather not know," Simms said. "That I'm a murderer."

"We'll cross one bridge at a time," Clark said. "Do we have your permission?"

"Yes."

"Good," Clark said. "I'll have the bodyguard drive you home."

"Bodyguard?" I said.

"That's right, you've been out of town," Clark said.

"I've been receiving death threats," Simms said. "A few phone calls and some messages on my answering machine. Some of them quite explicit and violent."

"Nuts coming out of the woodwork, but I've taken the precaution of assigning a bodyguard to Carly," Clark said.

"Maybe we should move her to an undisclosed location?" I said.

"To where?" Simms said.

"I'll make some phone calls," I said.

Simms nodded. She stood and walked to the door. Just before she opened it, she paused to turn around. She had the look of someone who knew the outcome ahead of time and what the consequences of that outcome would be.

"I can't imagine what that boy could have said or done to cause me to kill him," Simms said. "And I'm afraid to find out. God knows, I'm scared right down to my soul that I'm guilty."

"Don't be," Clark said. "I've kept the likes of Eddie Crist out of prison; I can do the same for you."

Simms nodded, opened the door and left.

There was a moment of quiet.

"She wasn't talking about being afraid of prison," I said.

Clark looked at me.

"I know," he said.

CHAPTER 25

I took a drive to see Jane and treated her to lunch. She had an urge for Chinese food. We took her cruiser to the Golden Palace Restaurant a few miles from the Public Safety Building.

As she slurped noodles with chopsticks, Jane said, "I hope to hell I'm not pregnant again. That damn useless husband of mine. Christ's sake, I'll be collecting Social Security when the damn kid is in high school."

I ate some fried rice using chopsticks. The best I could do was secure one grain. I switched out the sticks for a spoon.

"Ten years I've been telling the bastard to get it nipped," Jane said. "The son of a bitch, I swear to God I'll shoot it off if I'm knocked up one more goddamn time."

"Jane, any information on the laptop or those names?" I said, redirecting her attention.

Jane slurped some noodles before answering.

"Nothing on the laptop," she said. "I traced it back to the man who built it, but it hasn't been used since the Saturday morning Hughes was killed."

"That means he had it with him prior to meeting Simms," I said.

"Or he lent it to someone and they used it," Jane said. "And that is unlikely considering the thing cost about twenty grand with all the extra bullshit he had installed."

"It was worth a lot more than that with all his designs for new video games he had on it," I said. "I'm told he was so good at designing games, companies bid on his services. Somebody might be pissed off he wouldn't share."

"Throw a little corporate espionage into the defense to cloud the jury," Jane said. "Not bad, not bad at all, Bekker."

"Except that it might be true," I said. "Hughes was some kind of games design genius and his laptop held a lot of his own designs that could be worth millions in the right hands. Say, the hands of a competitor."

Jane nodded.

"I'll step up the search," she said.

"I've got to talk to a computer expert and find out how difficult it would be to pirate his information without getting caught," I said. "In the meantime, what about those names I gave you?"

Jane nodded and pulled a list from her shirt pocket. "Lunch is on you, right?"

"When I said I'd treat you to lunch, that was sort of the idea," I said.

"Just checking," Jane said. She squinted at the list. "Damn." She dipped into the other shirt pocket for reading glasses.

I ate some rice.

"The eyes go, you know you're middle-aged," Jane said. "What kind of mother is that for a newborn? Do you know how small the print is on baby food jars?"

"The list?" I said.

Jane perched the reading glasses on her nose. "No comments, please."

"The list?"

"Right. In the order you gave them to me," she said. "Michael Votto, 24, is living in Austin, Texas, and works at an art gallery where his own paintings are on display. Clean record. Stephen Stousser, 25, lives in the Twin Cities and attends the U of Minnesota where he plans to get his masters in accounting by next year. Clean record. Ty Butler, 24, serving the second year of a nickel stretch for armed robbery in Ohio. Scott Lind, 24, MIA for more than a year now. Joseph Buck, 24, lives in Denver where he is studying to be a pilot. Clean record. Josh Andrus, 23, clean record."

I sipped some tea as I thought for a moment.

"How hard did you look for Lind?" I said.

"Driver's license, Social Security record, arrest record, the usual."

"Did you check death records and obituaries?"

"No, no I did not," Jane said.

I sipped more tea.

"Must you look so fucking smug?" Jane said.

"Simms is getting death threats," I said.

"No surprise," Jane said. "Do you have a place to stash her?"

"Not yet."

"County has a witness protection safehouse, but good luck getting a judge to approve using it," Jane said.

"No, it's got to be something impervious to leaks," I said. "I'll think of something. Check death records for Lind and let me know."

"You want a lot for a free lunch."

"No such thing as a free lunch," I said. "Don't you know that?"

"I do now."

"I'll be at the lawyer's if you find anything."

"What about dessert?" Jane said.

CHAPTER 26

Frank Kagan is a tall, statuesque man in his early sixties. He was Eddie Crist's personal attorney for three decades before Crist passed away from cancer late last year. Kagan is what you would call semi-retired since Crist's death. Of course, when Crist was alive, Kagan was what you would call semi-employed, as the mob boss was his one and only client.

He seemed genuinely pleased to hear from me when I called him and asked if he could meet me at the office of David Clark.

Around five-thirty in the afternoon, Clark's secretary served coffee in his conference room while Kagan, Clark and myself waited for Carly Simms to arrive.

Clark and Kagan knew each other well, having overlapped many times on many occasions representing Crist's various interests. It would have been difficult for them not to. As Crist's criminal attorney, Clark's business often spilled into Kagan's world of personal attorney.

"What's happening with Crist's estate?" Clark said as he sipped coffee.

"Still working on the death and inheritance taxes," Kagan said. "It will go on for years, I'm afraid, but when all is said and done, it looks like the estate will pay about fifty-four million in total taxes to the IRS."

"And they said Crist was the criminal," Clark said.

"What about Campbell?" I said.

"As Mr. Crist's only surviving heir, she receives one million a year, plus she keeps his estate," Kagan said. "Taxes on both are to be paid by the estate, with the bulk of it going to various charities to offset some of the death tax penalties. Things will change when the estate is finally settled and she will benefit upon that as well."

There was a knock on the door. It opened and Carly Simms walked in, looked at us and closed the door. "Am I late?"

"Right on time," Clark said, "Please have a seat. Bekker has something he wants to ask you."

Simms sat opposite me at the conference table.

"I've been giving the death threats some thought and I've decided to play them for real and take no chances," I said. "That said, how would you like to move into a safehouse until this is over?"

"How long?" Simms said.

"From today until the trial, it could be as long as one year," Clark said.

Simms looked at Kagan. "Have we met?"

"No," Kagan said. "But if you're agreeable to this, we will be seeing a great deal of each other."

"If I'm agreeable to what?" Simms said.

"What I'm about to tell you to do," I said.

"Tell?"

"You don't have a lot of options," I said.

Simms nodded at me.

"I guess I don't," she said.

"Mr. Kagan is the personal attorney for the late Eddie Crist," I said. "I've made arrangements for you to live in his guest house at his estate until the trial. It's the safest place on Earth at the moment, with round-the-clock security and guards. The only other person at the estate is Campbell Crist, Eddie's daughter, and she lives in the main house."

"If I were worried about conflict of interest and my reputation, I would have a fit at the suggestion," Simms said. "Under the circumstances, I'm worried about neither. I agree."

"Excellent," Kagan said. "I'll have you moved first thing in the morning."

"What about Campbell Crist?" Simms said. "How does she feel about this?"

"Forty-two rooms in the estate, twelve in the guest house, I doubt you'll even run into each other," Kagan said.

Simms nodded. "I'm in no position to argue. I'll be ready in the morning."

"The other thing," Clark said. "Your session with the hypnotist, it's scheduled for next week on Tuesday at ten."

Simms nodded again. "Do I need to do anything, prepare anything for this?"

"All that's needed is for you to show up," Clark said. "No drinking or prescription drugs the night before. That's all there is to it."

"If we're done, I have a previous engagement," Kagan said.

"I'll walk down with you," I said.

Simms rode the elevator with us, along with her bodyguard.

At the curb where the bodyguard held the car door open for Simms, she paused to turn to me.

"From prosecuting criminals to taking their handouts," Simms said. "I've come full circle, haven't I?"

"Sooner or later, we all do," I said.

Simms nodded. "I guess you know about that," she said.

CHAPTER 27

By the time I arrived at my trailer, it was too late to swing by Janet's and mooch a free meal, so I fired up the grill and asked Oz to join me. As we listened to steaks sizzle on the grill and watched night slowly fall over the ocean, I gave Oz the lowdown on Regan's new developments.

"I guess I'll be the lone resident and keeper of the beach," Oz said. "You gonna sell?"

"I'm thinking of converting the trailer to an office," I said. "And hiring you part time to do clerical and take messages."

"Please tell me you're kidding," Oz said.

"I think it will work out fine," I said. "For both of us."

"Are you on the booze again?" Oz said.

"No, are you?"

"No."

"Good. Flip the steaks."

While Oz turned the steaks, I went inside to remove the pot of baked beans from the oven and set them on the counter to cool. I returned to my lawn chair with two mugs of coffee.

"What exactly would I have to do?" Oz said.

I grinned as I lit a cigarette.

"Answer the phone, set appointments, take messages, do research for me when needed, that kind of thing," I said.

"So we're talking what, twenty hours or so a week?"

"At least."

"How much you paying?" Oz said. "I don't want to bump my

pension into a higher tax bracket."

"Trust me, you won't."

"Then I'm your man," Oz said. "When you move out."

"Turn the steaks."

"If you make a fire," Oz said. "This time a year, eighty in the daytime, fifty at night, my arthritis can't take it."

I made a roaring fire in the trashcan that not only provided heat, but enough light for us to eat by. Down at the beach, the tide rolled in and the waves gave us music. I made coffee and served a dessert of layer cake from the freezer.

Eighty in the daytime, fifty at night, Oz said.

"Oz, I think you just earned your first paycheck," I said.

"For eating dinner?"

"For having arthritis."

"I see you're going to be a fun boss," Oz said. "Any more of this cake?"

CHAPTER 28

"Ever not see something even when you're looking right at it?" I said.

Walt cocked his head to look at me.

"I don't even know what that means," he said.

We were sitting in the rusty lawn chairs in front of my trailer, sipping coffee and watching the early morning sun sparkle over the ocean.

"Something's bothering me," I said.

"Really?"

"It's that damn heat being on in the motel room."

"The man stabbed to death and a state prosecutor as the likely murderer doesn't bother you, but the thermostat set a few degrees above government guidelines has you in a tizzy," Walt said.

I lit a smoke. Sipped some coffee. Don't let anybody tell you otherwise, there is no better combination than caffeine-fueled nicotine in the morning.

"I'm not in a . . . what the hell exactly is a tizzy, anyway?"

"It's you being a stubborn pain in the ass, is what it is."

"You're young, very fit and in a strange town," I said. "You're alone and single, looking for some action. Do you say to yourself, gee, it might get cold later, I better crank up the heat before you go out on the prowl?"

Walt took a sip from his mug and looked at me.

"Lots of possibilities," he said. "They get to the room and it's

111

cold. Simms turns up the heat all the way. They pass out or whatever and the room becomes an oven from the heat running all night. Or Hughes could have been the type of guy who checked the weather reports all the time, saw it was going to be a cold night and turned on the heat before he left the room. My father was like that when he got older, always fiddling with the heat."

"Maybe," I said. "But Hughes wasn't older, and if he used his laptop to check the weather, where is that laptop now?"

Walt took a sip from his mug.

"And where is Simms's .32?" I said.

Walt sighed. "Why do I get the feeling you're about to ask me something you shouldn't ask and I shouldn't listen to, but you will and I will," he said.

"Jane doesn't have the resources a big-city lieutenant does," I said. "She might maybe could use a little help on this."

"I thought that's what you were doing," Walt said. "Helping."

"Jane has little, but I don't have any resources at all."

"What the hell does might maybe mean?"

"See what you can come up with on the laptop," I said. "And the .32."

"Anything else?"

"Scott Lind."

"You don't mean the country that belongs to England, do you?"

"He's a person and he could be dead or he could be alive," I said. "I doubt he's both."

"Could you might maybe redefine that a bit?"

"Scott Lind was a friend of Jon Hughes from the orphanage," I said. "Along with some others. Jane did a search for me. Lind is the only one unaccounted for."

"And you want to know why."

"Missing pieces of a puzzle I don't have."

"Oh, well, that clears everything up for me," Walt said. "I assume you want ASAP on this."

"If you don't mind."

"Well, shit, I have nothing better to do," Walt said.

"Feel like another ride-along?" I said.

Walt shook his head. "I do have to give the taxpayers a little something for their money. I'll call you later."

"I'll be here later," I said.

CHAPTER 29

Campbell Crist didn't have what you would call a temper tantrum, but it was close enough that if she were a child it would merit a whack on the behind, no television and being sent to bed without dinner.

She yelled at Kagan that he couldn't bring someone into her home without her permission, especially someone who tried to put her father in prison and so on and so forth, mixing in a few choice four-letter words along the way.

Her tirade lasted fifteen minutes or so and ended when Kagan had enough and told her to shut up in no uncertain terms.

"Campbell, shut the fuck up," Kagan said. "In case you missed the reading of your father's will, I control your purse strings and I will do so until the day I'm gone, which, with a bit of luck, won't be for another twenty-five years. I can and will put your living expenses in a holding account for every one of those twenty-five years, so unless you want to be cut off and fending for yourself for the next quarter century, you will do as I say and shut the hell up about it."

Campbell Crist glared at Kagan.

"Now unless you two decide to schedule your sunbathing at the pool for the exact time every day, I doubt you'll even see each other," Kagan said.

Campbell Crist glared at Carly Simms.

"And, if you do this without incident, without bitching and moaning like the spoiled brat that you are, I'll have your yearly allowance bumped up two hundred and fifty thousand," Kagan said.

Campbell Crist glared at me. "You're that drunk cop," she said.

"I'm neither drunk nor a cop," I said.

Campbell dismissed me with a look and turned to Kagan. "I assume that 'without incident' means I keep my mouth shut that your femme fatale is living in the guest house."

"Correct," Kagan said.

"I guarantee you silence on my part for a five hundred thousand dollar a year raise in my allowance," Campbell said. "Otherwise, you can piss in the wind for all I care."

"One word leaks to the media, the prosecutor, Facebook or Twitter and you're on the street," Kagan said. "Are we clear?"

"Crystal," Campbell said. "And I wouldn't be caught dead on Twitter or Facebook."

"I'll take Miss Simms to the guest house," Kagan said.

"Any coffee?" I said to Campbell.

"In the kitchen," Campbell said. "Pour two and meet me at the pool. Oh, make mine espresso."

Campbell went one way. I went the other. Having been in the Crist mansion a dozen or so times, I was familiar enough with the layout to find the expansive kitchen. There were three types of coffee makers on the twenty-foot-long marble counter. Regular, espresso and cappuccino machine.

I made two large mugs of espresso, opened the sliding doors to the backyard and carried them poolside where Campbell was sunbathing in a lounge chair. She wore a deep blue bikini. Her tan was flawless. She was in excellent condition and had no problem putting it on display.

I sat in the lounge chair next to Campbell's, set the mugs on the small table between us and adjusted the back so I could sit up rather than lay prone.

Campbell looked at me and adjusted her chair to sit up. She reached for a mug and took a small sip.

"Not too bad," she said. "Light me a cigarette, would you?"

There was a pack of ultra-light cigarettes and a gold lighter on the table. I reached for both, lit one and gave it to her.

"I know what you think of me," Campbell said. "And I really don't care."

"If that were true you wouldn't mention it," I said.

Campbell turned her head to give me an icy stare.

"Okay, so what do I think of you?" I said.

"That I'm a spoiled forty-three-year-old rich bitch that spends her mornings on the Stairmaster, her afternoons at the pool and her evenings bedding young men."

"Except for the rich part, what's the difference between you and the woman in the guest house?" I said.

"I just fuck my men," Campbell said. "I don't stab them through the heart with letter openers."

"We don't know that she did that, either," I said. "That's what courts are for."

"How noble. Do my back," Campbell said.

There was a bottle of tanning lotion from Hawaii on the ground beside the table. I reached for it and opened the top.

Campbell turned in her chair and gave me her back.

"I usually have one of the trained talking monkeys from the gate do this," she said and removed the bikini top.

I squirted lotion on her back and started to rub.

"Did she do it?" Campbell said as she inhaled on the cigarette. "I ask because I'd like to know if I have a murderer under my roof."

"Like I said, I don't know," I said. "But I doubt you're in any danger."

"You don't like me, do you?"

"I don't know you."

"That's not what I asked."

I finished rubbing and reached for the towel on the back of the chair.

"Not so much, no," I said.

"And if you had been born the only daughter of Eddie Crist, would you have turned out any different than I?"

"That's not the reason I don't like you," I said.

Campbell turned to face me. Her breasts were as tanned as the rest of her.

"Oh?" she said. "Then by all means, fill me in."

"You're just not a likeable person," I said.

Campbell's face took on a hard look.

"Then I guess my houseguest and I have something in common after all," she said. "Have a nice day, Bekker."

Dismissed, I picked up my coffee and returned to the kitchen. As I walked away, I hear Campbell mutter, "Asshole," under her breath, but loud enough for me to hear.

I took a seat at the kitchen table.

I was on a second cup with a fresh cigarette when Kagan returned.

"She's settling in," Kagan said. "Do you need to see her before we leave?"

"No, but I would like you to stop off at Clark's office," I said. "It's on the way back and I won't be long."

Clark was working on a Motion of Discovery to the prosecutor's office when Kagan and I arrived.

"Simms is safely tucked away with little to no chance of a leak to the media," Kagan said.

"Good," Clark said. "Even though this might take a year, things are progressing quickly. The last thing we need is a media-fed death threat feeding frenzy."

"Something I've been thinking about," I said. "Which is why I stopped over. Carly Simms is not a likeable person. If trial were held today, she would come across as cold, callous and unfeeling to the jury. It's easier to give the death penalty to someone you don't like than someone who wins you over with charm and personality."

"That's been bothering me a bit, too," Clark said. "I've been wondering if it was just me?"

"It isn't," I said. "It's her. I know. I've known her a long time."

"There's someone I use to coach witnesses on the stand on how to make a good impression," Clark said. "I'll give him a call. We got a year to work with her, we might as well get started."

"One more thing," I said. "When Simms has her session with the hypnotist, I'd like to observe."

"So would I," Clark said. "I'll let you know."

I turned to Kagan.

"Feel like lunch?" I said. "I'll buy."

"Why not," Kagan said. "I think I've earned it."

CHAPTER 30

"I must admit, this isn't exactly what I had in mind when you said you'd buy me lunch," Kagan said. "But it is much more enjoyable than a crowded restaurant downtown."

His jacket, tie, shoes and socks removed, Kagan sat in Oz's rusty lawn chair and sipped iced tea from a tall glass. Ears of corn roasted on the grill. The trick was to soak them in cold water for fifteen minutes before tossing them onto the hot grill unshucked. Then, every ten minutes, turn them and wet them down from a water bottle. The steam brings out the natural sugar, sweetening the ears.

I had a mug of coffee from which I took a sip. "Something I want to talk to you about," I said as I lit a smoke.

"I figured that much," Kagan said. "This little elucidation of yours comes with a price. Well, I'm relaxed, happy and drooling over that corn, so now is a good time to broach your subject."

"It's about my daughter," I said.

"I figured that much as well," Kagan said. "She's doing better?"

"Extremely."

"Mr. Crist would have been very pleased to hear that."

"She's doing so well, her doctor believes she can live at home with me," I said.

"Here?"

"No. I'd buy a house or . . . find another arrangement."

"If you're wondering, the support money Mr. Crist left Regan is for life," Kagan said. "Even if she comes to live with you."

"What if I don't withdraw from it?"

"Oh, I see," Kagan said. "You're wondering what happens when you're no longer around and she's middle-aged. The answer to that is, the money will always be there for her for as long as she lives. Mr. Crist was very specific on that and the money he set aside is in a private account. Put your fears to rest about her financial future."

I got up to flip and water down the corn.

"How do you like your burgers?" I said.

CHAPTER 31

Fog rose off the ocean on a moonless, very dark night at the beach. I couldn't see the fog except in the headlights of an advancing car the moment the car turned off the street and onto the sand. It advanced slowly through the thick pea soup surrounding it, casting the headlight spill as eerie, yellowish beams.

I had time to go inside for a refill of coffee and to tuck the .45 I keep in the nightstand into the small of my back.

I returned to my lawn chair, lit a smoke and watched the car make a slow advance. Finally, the car arrived and shut down. Walt exited and walked to me.

"I saw you went inside," he said. "Stick the .45 in your back?"

"I did," I said. "Want some coffee?"

"Love some."

I fetched Walt a mug and he sat in Oz's chair.

"Ten at night, fog like a blanket, you must have something to tell me or you had a fight with your wife." I said. "Which?"

"Both."

"Which did you want to talk about?"

"Scott Lind is not among the missing," Walt said. "Scott Lind is among the dead."

"What's the other way to say that?"

"Scott Lind is among the murdered."

"I don't suppose you'd care to share the details?"

"Daytona Beach, last year during spring break," Walt said.

121

"That's what, in February?"

Walt nodded. "He's there with a hundred thousand other drunken college kids. Staying at the Beach Side Motel off the main drag. He was found beaten to death in his room by a housekeeper."

"Beaten?" I said. "How do you mean beaten?"

"According to the reports, beaten to a pulp," Walt said. "Cause of death was a brain hemorrhage, the kind boxers die of in the ring. Autopsy report showed he had one drink an hour or more before time of death."

"So he wasn't impaired."

"Seems so."

"Any witnesses?"

"Couple of shitfaced kids saw an old hooker leave Lind's room about two in the morning," Walt said. "They heard nothing like a fight after that."

"Got a description on Lind?"

"Six-two, two thirty," Walt said. "Played fullback in a semi-pro football league before enrolling in college. The story didn't get much air time since he had no family to sue Daytona. It went unsolved and got put on the Open Investigations list, where it sits untouched."

"So we got two men from the same orphanage murdered in motel rooms by older women?" I said. "Men much larger and fitter than average, one stabbed, the other beaten, and in each case an older woman was involved."

"Coincidence," Walt said. "I admit it's freaky, but still coincidence at this point."

I sipped, smoked and said, "What's your take?"

"Maybe he didn't want to pay the hooker?" Walt said. "She's got a bouncer type waiting in the wings who gets carried away collecting her fee."

"Could be," I said.

"Or?"

"Somebody is targeting these kids from the orphanage," I said.

"I knew you were going to say that," Walt said. "So let me point out a few things to you that may dampen your theory a bit. One year and twelve hundred miles of coastline separate the two incidents. One woman was a hooker, the other a state prosecutor. One victim was stabbed, the other beaten. One case has a suspect, the other does not."

"Granted," I said. "What are the similarities?"

"Both men are dead."

"Besides that," I said.

"Both men were murdered."

"From the same orphanage and in each case an older woman was involved."

"You're fishing for an angle to help Simms," Walt said. He wiped his brow, sipped some coffee, and looked at me. "Look, my marriage could go down the shitter if my affair with Simms comes out in open court. As a lifelong servant of the people, I would risk that if I thought it would do any good to fish for something in dead waters."

"Lifelong servant of the people?" I said.

"Okay, so maybe that's a little thick," Walt said. "But, you get what I'm saying. Reach too far for that brass ring and you risk falling off your horse."

"Your old tired clichés aside, suppose that I'm right and someone is targeting these kids from the orphanage," I said. "Do we wait until a few more are killed before we examine that possibility?"

Walt sighed.

I knew his sigh.

Nobody could sigh like Walt.

"I hate it when you're fucking right," he said.

"I'm not right," I said. "I just want to examine the possibility."

"While we're examining your possibility, what do you see as a possible motive?"

"It's a home for orphans and kids taken away from their parents, Walt," I said. "A hundred and sixty-eight at any given time. Could be one kid didn't fit in, wasn't allowed in a clique or a certain group, something like that. He's boiling over with rage and when he's old enough to go on his own, he starts taking revenge on those who scorned him."

"Scorned?" Walt said.

"Yeah, scorned, Mr. Lifelong Servant of the People," I said.

Walt mulled it over for a moment.

"You know, there might be something to that," he said.

"I think maybe I should get a list of names of the boys in that home during the time Jon Hughes and Scott Lind lived there," I said.

"Back to Utah?" Walt said.

"Wanna do a ride-along?" I said.

"The captain would never approve a trip like that without cause," Walt said. "And since this isn't even our case, there is no cause."

"The benefit of working in the private sector is I approve my own trips," I said. "With or without cause."

"When you going?"

"As soon as I talk to Clark."

"Let me know," Walt said. "Right now I got to go home or Elizabeth will have my ass."

"Tell her hi for me."

Walt stood up.

"Reminds me," he said. "She's still bugging me about you coming to dinner."

"When I get back from Utah," I said. "I'll make it a family outing."

Walt nodded. He walked to his car and opened the door.

"You never were afraid of falling off that horse, were you?" he said.

"No."

"I want to be like you when I grow up."

"Who says I'm a grown-up?" I said.

"Not me."

Walt entered his car. I sat there and watched his red taillights fade away into the fog and finally vanish into the darkness.

CHAPTER 32

"I have to admit I'm a bit surprised to see you again so soon," Brother Philip said to me as we sat down to coffee in the Sacred Heart dining room. It was mid-morning and the only other occupants of the hall were boys assigned to breakfast cleanup detail.

"Investigations have a way of coming full circle," I said. "Sometimes you just have to go along for the ride."

"What you said on the phone about Scott Lind being murdered, I find it really distressing," Brother Philip said. "That two of my boys died such horrible deaths long before their natural time."

"The police back home want to explore some possibilities," I said. "Can you put together a list of names of all the boys who were here during the same years as Hughes and Lind?"

"That will take some time," Brother Philip said. "A day at least."

"Time I got," I said. "Oh, and if you can remember who didn't like who or fights among the boys, it would be helpful. Especially any boy who might have reason to hold a grudge."

"Grudge?" Brother Philip said.

"For being kicked out of a group, picked on, ridiculed," I said. "The sort of thing that happens with teenage boys when they're forced to be together."

Brother Philip stared at me as he mulled that over. "I'll do my best," he finally said.

"I'm going to talk to the Andrus kid again," I said. "I'll be back in a few hours."

"You'll stay for dinner?"

"Wouldn't miss it."

Josh was just getting off duty at the TRAX Corporation and on his way to karate training when I showed up and offered to give him a ride. With his car still out of commission, he jumped at the chance to skip three bus rides and save a little fare money.

The thirty-minute drive gave us a chance to chat.

"Scott's dead?" Josh said after I filled him in on the latest.

"And Ty Butler's in prison," I said. "Five years for armed robbery."

"That one doesn't surprise me."

"Why?"

"Ty was always in trouble for stealing things at the home," Josh said. "We thought it was just kid stuff he'd outgrow, but I guess he didn't."

"No."

"Armed robbery means a gun, right?"

"Any dangerous weapon, but in his case, it does."

"He used to talk a lot about what he'd do when he got out," Josh said. "He always talked about getting a gun, but we never paid him much attention. Guys are always talking tough. Guess he was serious, huh?"

"Seems that way."

"Can I ask, I mean, how did Scott die?"

"He was beaten to death in a motel room during spring break in Daytona Beach."

"What do you mean beaten?"

"He took severe blows to the head like a boxer," I said. "When you get knocked out it's because the brain has been dislodged and free-floats a bit. If it's severe enough, you die from it. That's what happened to Scott."

"Jesus," Josh said. "Scott was a big guy. Played football. Who the hell could do that to him?"

"You've been studying karate a long time," I said. "I'll bet there are a few hundred-thirty pound guys in your class that could knock out a charging bull."

"Maybe, but we train for defense," Josh said. "Guys fight outside the gym or a tournament, Mr. Tilton kicks you out. No second chance. Just out."

"He's a disciplined man."

"I suppose," Josh said. "It's what he believes in. I guess we believe it, too, or we wouldn't train with him."

I turned into Tilton's parking lot.

I had the slip of paper at the ready.

"Josh, I'm going to give you my phone number at home and my cell," I said. "If you think of anything, anything at all, give me a call. If I'm unavailable, leave a message and I'll call you back. Okay?"

Josh took the slip and tucked it into his shirt pocket. "Sure."

As Josh opened his door, I could hear warm-up shouts from the students inside the gym. The word *discipline* came to mind.

I made it back to Sacred Heart in time for dinner.

Brother Philip and I shared a separate table near the kitchen. He had a legal pad between us and tapped it with his finger as he sipped coffee.

"More than seven hundred names," he said.

"That many?"

"It covers the eleven years Jon Hughes stayed with us."

"What about Scott Lind?"

"He was with us ten years, so there's an overlap between the two."

"Thank you," I said. "It may turn out to be a total waste of your time and mine, but I've got to look at everything. Sometimes you find something, most times you don't. I'm hoping this one is a don't."

"For the sake of Sacred Heart and all the boys living here, so do I," Brother Philip said.

"Any standouts on the list?" I said.

"You mean violent?"

"Not necessarily," I said. "Troubled, depressed, mentally disturbed. Anything like that?"

"At least twenty percent are troubled just by the fact they are without family," Brother Philip said. "Or family that cares."

I glanced at my watch.

"I have a ten o'clock flight home tonight," I said.

"Do you have time for dessert?" Brother Philip said. "Fresh baked apple cobbler with whipped cream and cinnamon."

"I think so," I said.

CHAPTER 33

The aroma of coffee brewing woke me up. My trailer is so small that any powerful aromas can linger for hours, sometimes even days. If I cook bacon and eggs on Monday, I can still smell the bacon come Thursday if I don't air the place out.

I sat up in bed and opened the blinds covering the small window. Janet and Oz were having coffee at the card table. I couldn't hear what they were chatting about, but Janet was laughing about something.

I tossed on my ratty old robe, filled a mug with coffee in the kitchen and went outside barefoot.

Oz and Janet turned to look at me.

"I've seen better-looking dead mice the cat dragged in," Oz said.

"There he is, that man of mine," Janet said.

I grabbed the third lawn chair next to Janet.

"I'm better after a shower, coffee and a few smokes," I said.

I eyed the card table. The pack of cigarettes I'd left there last night was suspiciously missing.

"I see you looking," Janet said. "And you won't find them."

"I have more in the . . ." I said.

"No, you don't," Janet said.

"The Marquis?"

"Nope."

"The cookie jar?"

"You don't have a cookie jar."

"I best be going home," Oz said.

"Oz, you sit there," Janet commanded. "He's less likely to hit a woman with you around."

"That means what, he's gonna hit me instead?" Oz said.

"What the hell's going on with you two?" I said.

Janet reached for a bag beside her left leg and set it on the card table.

"Because I love you," she said.

From the bag, she removed a smokeless cigarette starter kit that had a charger, smokeless cigarette tubes and one hundred and fifty refills.

"It's water vapor laced with nicotine and I got the full-flavored that you like so much," Janet said. "One is in the charger now. Try it."

I looked at the charger, which was loaded with a plastic stick.

"It won't bite and it's certainly less harmful than those chemical-laced bombs you smoke," Janet said.

I reached for the plastic tube in the charger, held it up and looked at it.

"Well, go on," Janet said. "Smoke the damn thing!"

I put the plastic tube to my lips and drew in warm, nicotine-laced water vapor. It wasn't the real thing, but it was close. When I exhaled, the vapor came out like smoke.

"Damn," Oz said. "What's next, men on the moon and color TV?"

Janet reached for another tube and put it in the charger.

"And that's all you do," she said. "Smoke one, have another charging."

Oz stood up.

"Well, I'm off to town," he said.

"I'll give you a lift," Janet said as she stood up.

"I thought after I took a shower, we'd . . ."

"You thought wrong, big boy," Janet said and kissed me on

the nose. "I have a twelve-hour shift ahead of me. But I can make a return trip after work, if you're up for it?"

I inhaled water vapor and nodded.

"Look at him, Oz," Janet said. "That man of mine."

"Looking at him hurts my eyes," Oz said.

Janet and Oz walked to her car. And off they went.

I finished my coffee and water vapor tube. I placed a new tube in the charger and then went in to take a shower to wash away last night's plane ride. I reemerged dressed in gym clothes, with a second mug of coffee and my cell phone.

I sat and dialed the number for Paul Lawrence, my old friend in Washington. More than a decade ago, he teamed with me on a RICO Act violation against Eddie Crist. Even though things went deep six and didn't work out, we've kept in touch.

I picked up the plastic tube and smoked water vapor while I was transferred to and fro before Lawrence came on the line.

"Bekker, how's things in your neck of the woods?" Lawrence said.

"Holding my own," I said. "You?"

"Same," Lawrence said. "So what favor do you want this time?"

I blew water vapor and sipped coffee.

"I hate being a foregone conclusion," I said.

"So who's dead or who's not, who's missing or who isn't?" Lawrence said.

"How much time you have?"

"Fifteen minutes."

"I'll give you the fourteen-minute version, then tell you what I need."

As I filled Lawrence in, I inserted another plastic tube into the charger. I talked as I smoked the tube and managed to wrap things up in twelve minutes.

"I met her a few times back then, didn't I?" Lawrence said.

"When the story hit cable last week, it took me a few minutes to make the connection. So, what do you need that I might be of some help with, that I know in advance I'll regret asking?"

"Like I said, two boys from Sacred Heart have been murdered. I'd like to check the list of names from the same time period and see what pops up."

"How many names?"

"Seven hundred or so."

"That's not a favor, that's a career."

"Come on, Paul. The FBI databank can do in ten minutes what would take the PD a month," I said. "And me a year."

"Once the names are entered into the system," Lawrence said.

"And you got people who do nothing but that."

"Who don't work for free, my friend," Lawrence said. "I want one dozen donuts from Pat's for me and two dozen for the crew who will work on your list. And I want them fresh and wrapped in plastic."

"Done."

"Fax me the list," Lawrence said. "I want the donuts by nine tomorrow."

"Isn't soliciting a bribe a crime?" I said.

"Sure is," Lawrence said and hung up.

I put another tube in the charger and stood up to crack my back. Too many plane rides takes its toll on old bones and mine are getting there. I went to the pull-up bar and cranked out a set. Then I dropped to the push-up bars and did reps until my arms and shoulders gave out. I repeated alternating sets until my upper body was inflamed, pumped and burning.

Then I went for a three-mile jog along the beach. I ran barefoot and it was slow going in ankle-deep water, but when I returned to the trailer, I felt pretty damn good about the way the morning was turning out, minus the vapor tubes.

Another shower to wash off the grime, I dressed in chinos and a shirt and walked the half mile to town with the list in my pocket. I retrieved the Marquis from the municipal lot and drove to the office supply store on the other side of town to fax the list to Lawrence.

From there, I drove to Pat's Donuts and had three dozen assorted shipped to the FBI Building in Washington in care of Paul Lawrence.

My day's work done, I took a ride over to see Jane.

CHAPTER 34

I took Jane for coffee to get her out of the office so we could talk in private. She asked for apple pie with a slice of melted cheese. I settled for a cup of coffee and brought her up to speed on my progress.

She raised an eyebrow as she sliced into her pie.

"Two dead and in similar fashion," she said. "What do you make of that?"

"Coincidence."

"Bullshit," Jane said. "No such thing and you know it. If you look for trouble, you'll find it every time. If you thought it was coincidence, you wouldn't have given the list to your FBI buddy, which, I might add, was the right thing to do. I have the manpower of a newsstand."

"Walt isn't much better off," I said.

"So what now besides waiting around for the FBI to get back to you?"

"I want to check out Room 15 one more time," I said. "Something is bugging me I can't put my finger on."

"I'll call dispatch and tell them I'm on cell," Jane said.

We took my Marquis.

Halfway to the motel, Jane suddenly looked at me.

"Pull over," she said.

"Why?"

"Just pull the fuck over."

I steered into the breakdown lane on the highway and slowed

to a stop. Jane shoved open her door, jumped out, stood bent over and barfed up apple pie. It took several good heaves for all of it to come up. Then Jane stood up and pulled a pack of tissues from her pocket to wipe her lips.

She took her seat and slammed the door.

"You okay?" I said.

"No," she said. "What I am is knocked up again and that's really fucking far from okay, that son of a bitch I'm married to."

I put the Marquis in gear and steered back onto the highway.

"Got some mints in the glove box to throw Janet off the scent," I said.

Jane flipped open the box and grabbed the roll of mints. "Does it work?"

"No. She's got the nose of a bloodhound."

"That fucking husband of mine, I swear to God, I'm going to cut it off," Jane said as she shoved a handful of mints into her mouth. "I'll be almost sixty when the kid starts high school."

"I saw a picture of Stallone in the paper recently," I said. "He's like sixty-four and has daughters in grade school."

"I'm not Sly Stallone and in case you . . . aw, fuck it. Got any smokes. I'm out."

"No. I got water vapor."

Jane looked at me.

"You've gone crazy, haven't you?"

I dug out the charger from my pocket and held it out to Jane.

"It's almost like the real thing," I said.

"So is wearing a condom, but will he listen?" Jane said as she reached for the plastic tube.

I placed another tube in the charger for me.

Jane sucked on the tube and exhaled.

"Water vapor," she said.

"You got twenty-plus years in, Jane, why not pull the pin?" I said.

"And do what, stay home and change diapers?" Jane said. "While I wait for my oldest to come home from college." She drew on the tube and blew out vapor. "This shit isn't half bad."

I picked up the charged tube and stuck it in my mouth.

"Maybe you can get me one of these things for my baby shower?" Jane said as she ate the last mint.

"Men don't go to . . . sure," I said.

I turned off the highway and headed to the Peek A Boo Motel. Ten minutes later, I parked in front of Room 15.

"I'll get the key," Jane said.

I charged up two tubes while Jane walked to the manager's office. I got out of the Marquis and stood in front of Room 15 to wait. As she returned with the key, Jane passed a vending machine beside the icemaker. She paused, then kicked the vending machine, then kicked it several more times until a pack of mints dropped out. She retrieved the mints and walked to me.

"I hate vomit breath," she said as she unlocked the door.

Room 15 was dark and cold.

I switched on the lights.

The AC unit hummed softly. With the shades drawn and sunlight unable to offset the constant running of the AC, the room was about fifty-eight degrees, a good twenty degrees cooler than outside.

"I could store dead fish in here," Jane said. "Or a dead husband."

I reset the wall thermostat to seventy-two degrees. It took a moment for the AC to shut down, then there was a soft click, followed by the low hum of hot air blowing through the vents.

"So what's bugging you?" Jane said.

"I don't know."

A little bit of dust blew out of the left vent above the bed. I turned and walked into the bathroom and clicked on the light. There was a ceiling vent and the warm air blew directly down.

I walked out and stood beside Jane.

The bed was bare to the mattress. Forensics had analyzed the blood and the covers and sheets were stored evidence.

"They get here at ten and the thump is heard around 1:30 in the morning," I said. "They didn't have sex, so besides polish off a bottle of wine, what else did they do for three-plus hours?"

"Watch TV? Talk? Maybe they were so drunk, they nodded off?" Jane said.

"The people next door reported no screaming or arguments before the thump," I said. "So maybe they did fall asleep."

"And she wakes up, panics and stabs him thinking she's being raped," Jane said.

"Then gets rid of her .32 and his laptop before passing out cold nude and covered in blood?" I said. "Why?"

"Hold that thought," Jane said. She raced to the bathroom and dropped to her knees in front of the toilet.

Between, "Good for nothing bastard," and "No good son of a bitch," Jane vomited several times before she finally stood up and rinsed her mouth at the sink.

She returned and shoved several of the stolen mints into her mouth. "You were saying?"

"The .32 and laptop are still big missing pieces of the puzzle," I said. "And for that matter, so is how they arrived here from the bar in their condition and without being seen."

"There's nothing on record at any cab companies," Jane said.

"Suppose the driver took them here off the meter?" I said. "And suppose Hughes had his laptop with him and left it in the cab. And suppose the .32 fell out of Simms's purse and the driver finds them both and decides to keep them?"

Jane nodded.

"That driver will keep the information to himself," she said.

"What if you circulated to the cab companies a ten thousand dollar reward for the return of both with no questions asked?" I said. "If we get the items back at least we know how they went from bar to motel."

"Whose ten grand?"

"Private money."

"I can put the word out."

I looked at the mattress. Dark circular patches of dried blood stained the lower half where Hughes had bled. The rug below was stained in similar fashion.

I sat on the mattress.

"Jane, I want you to sit on top of me," I said. "On my stomach."

"While you are cute and all, I'm a married, pregnant woman, Bekker," Jane said.

I stretched out and looked at Jane.

She climbed aboard.

"Now stab me in the chest," I said.

She stabbed down with empty hands.

"And get off."

Jane got off.

I rolled and allowed myself to hit the rug. My two hundred and twenty pounds landed with a soft thud.

Jane leaned over the mattress and looked at me.

"Would you be able to hear that from the next room?" I said.

"I barely heard that from this room," Jane said.

"Get the key for next door."

Ten minutes later, I talked to Jane on my cell phone.

"I'm going to roll off the bed," I said. "Tell me what you hear through the wall."

I set the cell phone on the nightstand and rolled from the bed to the rug. I landed with a soft thud, stood and picked up the phone.

"Jane?"

"I can tell you this much, Bekker," Jane said. "Whatever woke them up in here wasn't Jon Hughes hitting the floor."

"Come on back," I said.

Jane returned and we stood in front of the bed. She munched on a mint as we tossed things around.

"Nothing's broken," Jane said.

"And nothing's missing, according to the manager."

"What made that fucking thud?"

"Whatever it was, it wasn't Jon Hughes," I said.

"Got anymore of those vapor smokes?"

In between cycles, the AC unit kicked back on and a tiny bit of dust blew out of the left vent again. We watched the dust settle on the pillow below.

"If I had dust in my hair when I woke up, I'd demand my money back," Jane said.

"Hughes's body is still at the ME's?"

Jane nodded.

"There's nobody to claim it," she said.

"Ask the ME to check for dust particles in his hair," I said. "It might prove at least he got some sleep and account for some of the missing time."

Jane looked at me.

"When I grow up, I want to be just like you," she said.

"Walt said the same thing," I said. "Janet said I should just grow up."

Chapter 35

"Everyone, including myself up to this point, naturally assumed the thump the Atkinses heard was Hughes hitting the floor," Clark said. "Are you sure that it wasn't?"

"Positive," I said.

"And the dust particles?"

"The ME will let me know as soon as they test for it," I said. "Should have results by tomorrow."

"So what did the Atkins couple hear that woke them up?"

"Whatever it was, it wasn't Hughes or Simms hitting the floor," I said. "Those walls are thick enough to muffle anything except a direct blow to the wall."

Clark looked at me.

"I know," I said. "But there's no sign of a struggle. Not a thing out of place. Both of them drunk like that, it's a safe bet something got knocked over or broken if there was a fight before Simms stabbed him."

Clark nodded.

"The reward money?" he said.

"I called the TRAX Corporation," I said. "They would gladly pay ten grand to get Hughes's laptop back."

"Mysterious noises, missing laptops and revolvers. I must say, Bekker, this is turning out to be the mystery trial of the decade," Clark said.

"Is it enough to sway a jury?"

"No."

"What is?"

"Doubt and it doesn't have to be a lot of it."

"Do we have enough with the leaked polygraph test?"

"It's a start," Clark said. "Discrediting what the Atkinses heard goes a long way, too."

"What if her session with the hypnotist goes well, can we use that in court?"

"I'll render it to the judge and see what happens."

I sat back in my chair and looked across Clark's desk at him.

"There's something else going on here," I said.

Clark nodded.

"Let me know if you figure it out," he said. "Just don't take too long or a jury will hand down the death penalty."

CHAPTER 36

"Why are you going to Ohio in the morning?" Janet said as she snuggled her face in my chest. Her nose was cold. I wasn't sure if she was being affectionate or using me as a nose warmer.

I decided on affectionate.

"Talk to a prisoner who knew Jon Hughes," I said.

"Will it do any good? Seems to me he couldn't have anything to do with it from a jail cell."

"That's true."

"But you're going anyway?"

"You never know what someone knows until you ask them," I said.

"Does that go for everybody?"

"Yes."

"Me?"

"Yes."

Janet sat up in bed. Her forty-seven-year-old body was all lean muscle from a lifetime of daily runs and proper diet. Veins ran down her well-defined biceps to her wrists.

"For instance, I'm going to ask you what's on your mind," I said. "Because it certainly isn't Jon Hughes."

"You've been a cop too long."

"I haven't been a cop for thirteen years."

Janet tapped her naked chest over her heart.

"In here," she said. "You'll always be one."

"I don't think you want to talk about me being a cop," I said.

"No."

On the nightstand beside the bed was the charger with a fresh tube. I reached for it, inserted a new tube into the charger and inhaled water vapor.

"I sit in the background and quietly observe," Janet said. "And what I see is a man not ready for a family. It's off to Utah or Ohio because there's one more bad guy you haven't locked up yet. Regan needs her father. How can she depend on you when you're always off playing super cop and never around?"

I inhaled on the tube and exhaled water vapor.

"It's not like money is such an issue that you need to hire yourself out like the gunslinger in the old west," Janet said. "So tell me please what the fascination is all about that you feel the need to play Sam Spade for a living?"

"It's not a fascination," I said. "And it's Paladin."

"What is?"

"The hired gunslinger. That was his name. Paladin."

"Never mind his name," Janet said. "Tell what it is if not a fascination."

I took a sixty-second timeout to examine my life. The wheels spun and the years raced by to the only conclusion they could arrive at.

It wasn't pretty.

"This is all I know how to do," I said. "I don't know anything else."

"That isn't what frightens me," Janet said. "What does is that what you do is who you are."

"That isn't true."

"No. Separate the two and tell me what's left over?" Janet said. "Go on, I'll wait."

Like I said, it wasn't pretty.

"What would you have me do?" I said. "Collect my little pension and work part time in a store somewhere? I can't reinvent the wheel at my age."

"Look at me, you stupid prick," Janet said.

I looked at her.

"For the first time since she's a little girl, your daughter is showing real progress," Janet said. "Think about what would happen to her if you went and got yourself killed on one of your adventures. Then tell me it's all you know how to do."

Argue with a woman who is heads and tails smarter than you and you'll lose every time.

"Okay," I said.

"Okay, what?"

"I'll find something else to do, but I have to finish this," I said. "I love my daughter and I love you and Mark. All three of you are more important to me than playing private eye and it would kill me to lose you. I want to say we should talk about becoming a family, but I think we already are. You told me to think about getting married and I have thought about it and I'm ready for it if you are."

Janet placed her right hand to her ear.

"Do you hear that?"

"What?"

"The sound of hell freezing over."

"I'm serious," I said.

"I know you are," Janet said. "At the moment. Let's put the big M discussion for after you've completed your work on this case, then we'll talk about it. I don't want you making rash decisions you'll regret later on."

"The only thing I'll regret later on is us not becoming a family if we don't become one," I said.

Janet placed her head on my chest.

"How are those vapor cigarettes?" she said.

I set the empty tube on the nightstand.

"Not too bad," I said. "Could use some garlic, though."

"Want me to drive you to the airport in the morning?"

"Mark at his father's?"

"Yes."

"Only if you promise to pick me up," I said.

Janet kissed me on the lips.

"You are a very cheap date," she said.

"That's because I've never learned the secret of making money," I said.

Janet was suddenly on top of me and frisky as hell.

"There is more to life than money," she said. "Here, I'll give you a demonstration."

Argue with a woman who is smarter than you and you'll lose every time.

Some arguments are worth losing.

CHAPTER 37

The maximum-security prison in Manchester, Ohio, was as good a place as any to serve hard time. It was large, modern, clean and efficient. Prisoners were well cared for, were able to work a paying job or attend educational classes and had plenty of downtime to exercise in the yard, read in the library or watch cable television.

The visitors' center was one large room with eight doors and a guard at each door. There were eight tables for inmates to visit loved ones. Three other tables besides the one I sat at were occupied. I waited fifteen minutes for Ty Butler to arrive.

A door opened and a guard escorted him into the room. The guard pointed to me and Butler sauntered to the table. He was a runt of about five six or seven, a hundred and forty pounds. He wore a white tank top with prison pants and boots without laces. A red bandanna held his shoulder-length hair back off his face. A dagger dripping blood covered his left forearm. The face of Jesus covered his right shoulder. He looked to me to be a punk. I rarely judge a book by its cover, but sometimes the title says it all.

He slid out the chair and flopped down. "Who the fuck are you?"

I removed my wallet and showed him my ID.

"So?" Butler said. "I don't know you. What the fuck you want?"

"Talk," I said. "About Sacred Heart and Jon Hughes."

"My price for agreeing to talk to you is one carton of cigarettes," Butler said. "Marlboro Reds. Can you do that?"

"I can do that," I said.

"My price for actually talking to you is two cartons."

"Agreed."

"Before you leave here," Butler said. "There's a store in the lobby when you come in. You buy them and give them to a guard in my name."

"Anything else?" I said.

"A woman would be nice."

"That I can't do unless they sell them in the lobby store."

Butler allowed himself a tiny grin.

"So now we got a price settled, what the fuck you want?"

"You grew up at Sacred Heart with Jon Hughes and Scott Lind," I said. "Do you remember them?"

"Yeah, I remember them," Butler said. "A couple of pussies. What about 'em?"

"They've both been murdered."

"So?"

"So tell me what you know or remember about them."

"Mother fucker, I didn't kill them," Butler said. "What fucking difference it make what I remember?"

"It's how a police investigation works," I said. "Fill in the blanks, that kind of thing. I'm trying to establish what kind of men they were."

"Pussies," Butler said. "That kind."

"Fair enough," I said. "Why?"

"Why they're pussies?"

I nodded.

"Big guys like you think 'cause they're big, it makes them tough," Butler said. "It don't. Those two always playing sports, doing karate, a couple of queers if you ask me."

"Football and karate means you're gay?" I said.

"Hair gel and whacking each other in the ass with towels in the locker room does," Butler said. "Even if they don't know it."

"Latent?"

"Whatever," Butler said. "What that mean, latent?"

"Repressed feelings."

"Like when the prison shrink asks me how I feel about my mother?"

"Yeah. How do you feel about your mother?"

"Fuck her, man," Butler said. "Old whore dumped me in a fucking home when I was just a baby. She's probably dead or a crack ho by now. Who gives a fuck?"

"What about Hughes and Lind?" I said. "They ever talk about not having parents?"

"Shit, man. Everybody in the place talks about that. It's why we in that shithole to begin with, 'cause our parents dumped us or fucking died."

"Tell me about Hughes," I said. "What kind of a kid was he?"

"The kind always a pain in the ass, that kind," Butler said. "Always with that karate shit, thinking he better than everybody else. He weren't. He just like the rest of us homeless mutts nobody wants."

"I heard different," I said.

"Yeah, what you hear?"

"I talked to Brother Philip," I said. "He told me Jon Hughes always spoke highly of you. Jon would visit the home and give Brother Philip updates on his friends. How do you think I got your name?"

"Brother Philip is smoking crack," Butler said. "I haven't seen Hughes since the day I left that dump. Same for that other pussy Lind."

"Do you think Brother Philip got you mixed up with another boy?"

"Fuck, man, ask him," Butler said. "He nothing but an old queer, you ask me."

"Is there anything else you can tell me about Hughes or Lind?"

"Like what?"

"Anything. Their personal habits? What they wanted to do when they got out? Whatever you remember."

"I already told you . . . no, you know what," Butler said. "That Hughes was always fucking around with computers in the library. Said he wanted to go to college or some shit and study them when he got out. You ask me, he was checking porn sites for young boys."

"And Lind?"

"He was always talking that college shit, too, but I don't know for what."

"What about girls?"

"It's an all boys home, what about them?"

"Did they ever talk about them?"

"You think a bunch of sixteen year-old boys locked up talk about anything else?" Butler said. "Pussy and sports is all you talk about."

"What about Josh Andrus, do you remember him?"

"Oh, yeah, I remember him," Butler said. "Biggest pussy of them all. Used to follow Hughes around with his head up his ass. Took karate with him, probably took showers with him, too."

"One more question," I said. "Call it a bonus round. I'll throw in three extra cartons of cigarettes if you can tell me why Brother Philip gave me your name as being an old friend Hughes kept in touch with after you got out."

"Means five cartons?"

"That's what it means," I said. "For an honest answer to my question."

Butler stared at me for the longest time. His eyes never moved. His weight never shifted. His body didn't fidget. His shoulders didn't slump.

"I don't know," he finally said.

"Five cartons will be in your cell by the time you return," I said.

"Hey," Butler said. "You find out what's going on, you let me know."

"Sure."

Five hours later, Janet picked me up at the airport. I slid into her car and she greeted me with a kiss.

"Did you ask your questions?" she said.

"Yes."

"Did you learn anything?"

"I learned that someone is lying through their teeth."

"About?"

"I have no idea," I said. "Yet."

CHAPTER 38

The guards at the gate to the Crist Mansion were familiar enough with me now that they no longer felt the need to frisk me or even ask if I was armed. I wasn't. I drove through to the cul de sac in front of the mansion.

I rang the front doorbell.

A housekeeper answered and told me the ladies were sunbathing by the pool.

I took the long way around by the garden path to the rear of the house where the pool was located. There were lounge chairs for forty. Just two were occupied.

Campbell Crist.

Carly Simms.

Side by side.

I wasn't sure if they were asleep behind their sunglasses until I was less than twenty feet from them. Both were topless. Campbell was exceptionally tanned. Simms was not.

I knew they were awake when Simms sat up and reached for a towel to cover her upper body.

Campbell didn't so much as budge.

"I see you're working on your tan," I said to Simms.

"I'm trying to relax before tomorrow," Simms said. "Campbell has been a big help. A godsend."

"Really?" I said.

"Birds of a feather, Mr. Bekker," Campbell said. "Are bitches that stick together."

"Feathers aside, I need a moment of your time," I said.

"Me, or us?" Campbell said.

"I didn't drive all this way to admire your tanned breasts," I said.

Campbell stood up and walked to the edge of the pool.

"Play nice, you crazy kids," she said and dove into the water.

I took Campbell's chair.

"She really has been very nice," Simms said. "I have to admit."

I cocked an eye to the pool where Campbell had started swimming laps. "Really?"

"Surprised the hell out of me, too," Simms said.

"I have a message from Clark concerning your session with the hypnotist tomorrow," I said.

"He couldn't call?"

"Sure, but I told him I wanted to see how you were doing, anyway."

"And how am I doing?"

"I hope you remembered sunscreen."

Simms allowed a tiny smile to cross her lips. "I thought we were alone."

"You were until I showed up."

Simms reached for a pack of cigarettes on the table between the chairs. She lit one and looked at me. "So what's the message?"

"It's from the psychiatrist, actually," I said. "No alcohol or drugs for at least twelve hours before the ten a.m. session tomorrow, unless they're prescription and absolutely necessary. No coffee or caffeine products six hours before the session. Try to get eight hours' sleep. No vigorous exercise in the morning and have a light meal for breakfast. No smoking or drinks with caffeine one hour before the session."

"And what does he want me to wear?" Simms said.

"The idea being no stimulation to throw off the session," I

said. "I think what you wear doesn't matter."

"I know. I was being a wise ass."

"I know and I fully understand."

"Do you?"

"I'm a drunk," I said. "I know what it feels like to look into your own soul and not like what you see."

Simms nodded.

"I guess you do," she said.

"We won't be allowed in the room, but Clark and I will observe on monitor if you give your permission," I said.

"I don't see why not," Simms said. "You know every other damn thing about me at this point, including what my tits look like."

"Hey, don't forget that great ass shot," I said.

Gallows humor has its place.

This was one of them.

Simms rewarded me with a tiny smile.

"So, I'll see you tomorrow," she said.

"Sure."

I stood up.

"Hey, Bekker? I'm really scared. At what I might find out."

"I know."

I left thinking, aren't we all scared of the same exact thing? The one person we can never hide from is the one who looks back at us in the mirror.

That guy.

CHAPTER 39

I sat in my rusty lawn chair and watched the fire in the trashcan as it provided light and much-needed warmth. This afternoon topped out at seventy-nine degrees, but heavy fog rolled in and by dark, it dropped to the mid-fifties.

The breeze off the ocean made it feel ten degrees lower than that.

I wore a ratty gray sweatshirt and zipped it up as I sipped coffee from a mug. There was a tube in the charger. I grabbed it and inserted another.

Ty Butler was a lying little weasel of a human being. He was destined to spend most of his life in one prison or another, or die young. It was written all over him. For one thing, he wasn't smart enough to learn from his mistakes. For another, he envisioned himself a gangster, someone to be admired by fellow inmates and peers on the outside.

Except that he didn't lie when I asked him why Brother Philip said Hughes told him he kept in touch over the years.

As a cop, you're trained to spot a lie when interviewing a suspect.

They look to the left when remembering, the right when making something up. They fidget to release nervous tension built up from their lies. They tug at their ears or scratch their nose as blood fills tiny vessels there when anxiety builds from their lies. After a while, a liar will grow defeated and slouch in his chair. An innocent man's anger will grow under questioning.

A liar's anger will fade quickly as the energy used from sustaining the lie drains all his strength.

It's at that point a trained investigator switches the interview to an interrogation. It's at that point a confession comes quickly and easily as the subject is defeated.

That point never came with Ty Butler.

So if Butler was telling the truth, was Brother Philip lying?

Someone was.

I made the mistake of not putting myself in interrogation mode when I met with Philip at Sacred Heart. I hadn't felt the need to treat the Brother as a suspect and put him on the defensive.

I still don't.

Josh Andrus said he knew those boys, but didn't keep in touch with them. He said, knowing Jon, it didn't surprise him that Jon would.

It was beginning to appear that Jon Hughes might be the liar in the group.

Why?

What was there to gain by telling Brother Philip tall tales about former residents of Sacred Heart?

Maybe I was looking at it backward.

Maybe there was nothing to gain?

Maybe there was something to lose?

I couldn't confront Jon Hughes or Scott Lind.

I could pay a visit to Michael Votto, Stephen Stousser and Joseph Buck.

It was the only way to determine if Jon Hughes was less than truthful to Brother Philip and maybe find out why.

I packed it in and decided to get to bed early.

Constructed of aluminum, the trailer was usually ten degrees cooler than the outside temperature. The heat was generated by hot air blown through vents in each room. I set the thermostat in the kitchen to sixty-eight degrees to get the chill out before settling into bed.

I was still in the kitchen when the blowers kicked in and a sprinkling of dust blew out of the vent in the ceiling to the floor.

I sat at the table and smoked a vapor tube while the kitchen warmed.

That little something started to nag at me again.

Sometimes in a complicated investigation, teams of detectives are assigned specific parts of the investigation to work on. It prevents a detective from being overloaded with too much information. When facts, clues, evidence, witness statements, forensics all come together in a blur, assigning specific parts to a team prevents overload.

That's what was happening to me now.

Overload.

The kitchen started to warm up a bit.

Some more dust blew out of the vent and settled on the floor.

My eyes went to the floor, to the dust.

Slowly, my focus shifted from the floor to the vent in the ceiling.

"Yeah," I said aloud.

CHAPTER 40

Clark and I sat at a table in the conference room at Dr. Clifford Young's and watched the television monitor that rested between us. It was 21-inch and HD. The picture was perfect with resolution so clear I could almost read the time on his watch as he talked to Simms in his office. A red light on the DVD player indicated the session was being recorded.

Simms wore comfortable blue jeans, a white, button-down shirt and black walking shoes. She appeared relaxed and comfortable, at least on television.

Young was a very tall man in his fifties. His white hair was neatly cut and combed. Rimless glasses perched on his nose. His bright blue eyes shone with intelligence and compassion.

If Hollywood put out a casting call for a movie psychiatrist, Young would fit the bill to a tee.

"How do you feel, Miss Simms?" Young said.

His voice had a soothing quality that didn't sound practiced.

"Fine, all things considered," Simms said.

"Good, good," Young said. "Are you ready then?"

"Yes, I suppose so."

"Good. So we'll explore some things and see where that takes us."

Simms nodded.

"Now, what I'd like you to do is close your eyes and relax," Young said. "Concentrate on my voice. Listen to how soothing my voice sounds to you. How much it relaxes you. Can you hear how relaxing my voice is to you?"

"Yes," Simms said with eyes closed.

"How each word I speak makes you feel more and more relaxed," Young said.

"Yes," Simms said.

Young reached over to his desk for a pencil. He held it by the tip.

"Now what I'd like you to do is open your eyes and focus on this pencil," Young said. "On the eraser. Can you do that?"

"Yes."

"Open your eyes."

Simms opened her eyes.

"Do you see the eraser?"

"Yes."

"Focus on the eraser," Young said. "You see nothing else but the eraser and hear nothing else but my voice."

For ten minutes, Young continued to put Simms deeper and deeper into a hypnotic sleep. He tested her state of mind with childhood questions and asked her to act out some of her experiences.

Satisfied Simms was as far under as she was going to go, Young took her back to the Saturday of the incident. He lowered the pencil, told her to close her eyes again and relax.

"It was Saturday, yet you were at the office," Young said. "Is that normal?"

"When the cases pile up," Simms said. "There have been times where I've worked an entire month without a day off."

"Tell me what happened after you left the office," Young said.

"I was driving home," Simms said. "The Watering Hole Bar is on my way. I decided to stop for a glass of wine and unwind a bit."

"Have you been there before?"

"Yes, on occasion. Usually on my way home. Maybe once or

twice a week."

"Okay, so you stopped for a glass of wine," Young said. "What happened next?"

"I finished my glass of wine and was about to leave when this very cute young man asked if he could buy me another," Simms said. "Wait, that isn't right. The wine arrived first, then he came over to talk to me."

"Then what happened?"

"We started talking and had several more glasses of wine," Simms said. "He said I had great legs. I thought he was really cute."

"Were you drunk at this point?" Young said.

"Yes, but not so far gone I didn't know what was happening."

"And what happened?"

"He asked me if I would go back to his hotel room with him."

"And did you?"

"Not right away," Simms said. "We had a few more glasses of wine first. My head was spinning when we left the bar. I guess I was really drunk by then."

"Do you remember what time that was?"

"No."

"And how did you go from the bar to the motel?"

Simms hesitated. Her brow wrinkled. She was thinking, remembering.

"I don't . . . we . . . there was a car," she finally said. "It drove us."

"A taxi?"

"It wasn't metered. It was . . . I think it was private," Simms said.

"A gypsy cab?"

"I think so, yes."

"You arrived at his motel room and then what happened?"

"We kept drinking wine."

"You had a bottle?"

"It was in the room."

"You finished the whole bottle?"

"I don't know. Maybe."

"Then what happened?"

"Hot. I was so hot. We took our clothes off in the bed. He was sweating. So was I. I felt as if I couldn't breathe."

"Did you make love?"

"No."

"Why not?"

"He . . . fell asleep."

"Passed out?"

"Maybe."

"And you?"

"I fell asleep or passed out soon afterward."

"Did you wake up at all before the police arrived?"

"No," Simms said. "Wait. I . . . remember something."

"What do you remember?"

Simms started breathing hard as if suddenly filled with anxiety. Young picked up on her change right away.

"Relax, Miss Simms," he said. "No one will harm you."

Simms started to hyperventilate.

"Miss Simms, can you hear me?" Young said.

"Yes."

"I want you to relax," Young said. "Completely relax and go limp. Breathe softly and allow all of your muscles to relax."

Slowly, Simms relaxed and went limp in her chair.

"Now tell me what you remember that upset you so," Young said.

Simms raised her hands in front of her body as if holding something. Then, in a jerking motion, she stabbed downward with clasped hands. Her breathing increased until she was out of breath and gasping for air.

"That's enough," Young said. "Relax."

Simms went limp again.

"Did you stab that man?" Young said.

"Yes."

"Why?"

"I don't know why. I just did."

I looked at Clark.

Clark sighed and looked at me.

"Now what?" I said.

"In the most legal of terms," Clark said, "we're fucked."

CHAPTER 41

To her credit, Simms never so much as flinched when she watched the session on the television in Young's conference room.

We drank coffee as the one-hour session played out.

When the television finally went blank, Young used a remote to turn it off and we sat in silence for a moment.

Simms spoke first.

"I guess . . . that's it then," she said. "I'm guilty. I killed that man as the evidence suggests."

"Suggests does not necessarily mean ironclad," Clark said. "Remember O.J."

"You want I should start wearing a bloody glove?" Simms said. "It's obvious I stabbed him. It will be obvious to a jury that I'm guilty."

"Let me worry about the jury," Clark said.

"And what should I worry about, the death penalty?" Simms said.

"No, worry about the expense money I'm going to ask you for when I drive you home," I said.

Simms and I left Clark and Young to watch the DVD of the session one more time. I'm sure Clark had questions for Young's ears only.

In my car, Simms smoked a cigarette and stared out the window.

She finally looked at me. "What expense money?"

"Couple of plane tickets to interview some loose ends," I said.

"I suppose I should start paying my bills," Simms said.

"Don't crack open the piggy bank just yet," I said. "I'm running a tab on Visa."

"Bekker, can we stop somewhere for a drink?" Simms said. "I could really use a shot. Oh, I'm sorry. I shouldn't have . . ."

"Not wanting to disappoint my daughter keeps me sober," I said. "Not staying out of bars. I could get drunk at home anytime I want, if I wanted."

Simms nodded.

I found a quiet bar downtown where Simms had a tall glass of white wine to my tall glass of ginger ale on ice.

"What I can't figure out is why the hell I would do such a thing," Simms said. "Unless drunk is a motive, I stabbed him for no apparent reason."

I sipped ginger ale.

"Maybe Clark can sweet-talk a jury out of the death penalty, but not life without parole," Simms said. "I've stood before enough juries to know how they will think and vote just by the look in their eyes."

"Mind a few questions?" I said.

"Mind a lack of viable answers, because that's all I've got."

"Do you remember being under hypnosis?" I said.

Simms nodded.

"What did it feel like?"

Simms took a sip of wine.

"Like I was wide awake and asleep at the same time," she said. "Like that dream you have every once in a while where you're dreaming that you're awake. It's the only way I can describe it."

"Now that it's over, do you remember killing Jon Hughes?" I said.

"No."

"What do you remember?"

"Nothing."

"About stabbing Hughes?"

"Not a thing," Simms said.

"You know what the prosecutor will say?"

"Sure," Simms said. "That I was in an alcohol-induced blackout when I murdered him. What I want to know is how Clark will respond to that?"

"Ever been that drunk before?"

"At least two bottles of wine on an empty stomach, no," Simms said. "I'm usually a light drinker and cut myself off at three."

I polished off my ginger ale.

"I'll get you home," I said.

The late afternoon sun was bright and warm when we arrived at the Crist mansion gates.

"Wait for me by the pool," Simms said. "I'll be right out with a pot of coffee."

I walked around the mansion to the pool where Campbell was prone on a lounge chair. For once, she wasn't topless and sat up when she heard me approach.

"How did out little femme fatale perform under pressure?" she said.

I took the chair next to Campbell.

"If you mean how the session went, that's a matter of opinion," I said.

"That sounds intriguing," Campbell said. "Tell me more."

"I'm afraid it's confidential."

"Worried I might tip off the opposition?"

"No," I said. "Simms is my client and I owe her confidentiality. If she wants to, she can tell you herself."

Campbell laughed, showing perfect teeth that at some point

must have set her father back forty grand or more.

"She hasn't paid you a dime yet, has she?" Campbell said.

"I'm not worried about it," I said.

Campbell stood up.

"I'll be right back," she said and walked into the house.

I pulled out the charger from my pocket, removed a tube and placed it between my lips. Before I tucked it away, I slipped an empty tube into the charging slot.

Simms came around the side of the house with a tray in her hands. It held coffee pot, creamer and mugs. She set the tray on a table between the chairs.

"Let me know if you want the real thing," Simms said. "I have a fresh pack."

Simms filled two mugs with coffee, opened the cigarettes, sat and lit one.

"Once you get used to the idea it's water vapor instead of smoke, these aren't half bad," I said.

"Sure," Simms said. "And once you get used to the idea, a blowup doll is the same as a real woman."

"What is the same as a real woman?" Campbell said as she came up behind me.

"Vapor cigarettes," Simms said.

Campbell took her seat. "You need to get out more, Mr. Bekker." She held her right hand out to me. In it was a check.

"For your expenses," Campbell said.

"Wait a minute," Simms said. "I won't have you or anybody else paying my way. I can afford to pay for . . ."

"Bekker has places to go and people to see in the cause of helping you," Campbell said. "You can't expect him to keep spending his own money, can you? Besides, call it a loan if you must. Truth is, because of you, my allowance has increased a half million a year. I think I can spend a few thousand as a show of gratitude."

I looked at the check. It was for twenty-five thousand.

"Let me know when you need more," Campbell said.

I picked up a mug and took a sip of coffee.

"Never play with dolls when you can play with the real thing," Campbell said.

CHAPTER 42

From my rusty lounge chair, I watched the sun slowly dip below the horizon. I had a mug of coffee and a charged vapor cigarette for company. Oz would be along any minute now with a bag of steaks, but for the moment, I was alone with my thoughts.

In front of a jury, Simms was guilty. It came down to the death penalty or life without parole. Both were the same thing. One just took longer to reach the same conclusion.

Somebody was a liar.

Jon Hughes?

Brother Philip?

Ty Butler?

When I returned to the trailer from the Crist mansion, I called Young and asked him if there was any chance Simms faked her session.

None, was Young's answer.

Then he had a question of his own. Wouldn't Simms fake her session to appear innocent, if she was going to fake it?

I agreed and said goodnight to Young.

I called Clark at his office.

He said that although things weren't looking so good at the moment, news of Simms's polygraph exam would be leaked within a few days. Once it was known that she passed, it would stir up some sympathy with the public. After all, he said, the public does sit on a jury.

"You watched the session a second time," I said. "Did you

see anything different?"

"If by different you mean did I see anything to convince me she's innocent, my answer is no," Clark said.

"The motive is what bothers me," I said.

"You mean lack of," Clark said.

"Can you use that, lack of motive?"

"Right now, my entire case revolves around it," Clark said.

I sat for a while after speaking with Clark and smoked another vapor tube.

A bit later Paul Lawrence called from Washington.

"Sixteen from that list are on active duty in the military," Lawrence said. "Eleven are deployed in war zones. Ten are doing time in various prisons around the country. The bulk of the names check out. Most are gainfully employed, have clean records and many have families of their own."

"You said most," I said.

"You're the kid who sneaks a peek at his new bike behind the water heater before Christmas, aren't you?" Lawrence said.

"What have you got?" I said.

"Thomas Sutton and Robert Maggio," Lawrence said.

"And they are?"

"What they are is a stockbroker and a firefighter," Lawrence said. "What they are is a resident of Portland, Oregon and Seattle, Washington. What they are not is alive."

I sat up in my chair.

"Murdered?" I said.

"See that new bike yet?"

"In motel rooms?"

"Looks shiny. Don't it?"

"How?"

"Sutton in a motel outside of Portland seven months ago," Lawrence said. "County sheriff's jurisdiction. Let's see, how did he put it? Oh, yes, Thomas Sutton was just sort of beat up to death. Robert Maggio was stabbed through the heart in a motel room north of Seattle eleven months ago. State police handled that one. Both cases are still active, but in the open file."

"Women?"

"Ah, the prize," Lawrence said. "The new bike comes with a shiny new bell."

"Let me guess," I said. "Two cougar types were found dead with them."

"Cougar meaning middle-aged women of the sexy type who like younger men?"

"I don't mean the Pink Panther."

"Correct on both accounts."

"How?"

"Both women were strangled to death."

"Found with Sutton and Maggio?"

"Again, correct."

"What about Michael Votto, Stephen Stousser and Joseph Buck?" I said.

"Let me check the list," Lawrence said.

That gave me time to switch out the spent tube for the one in the charger and stick in another.

"Alive and well as far as I can determine," Lawrence said when he came back on the line. "Votto got a parking ticket six months ago. That's about it. Why these three?"

"Their names were given to me by the Brother who runs Sacred Heart as being close friends of Jon Hughes," I said. "I was thinking of going to talk to them, check out their stories."

"Before something happens to them?"

"That has occurred to me," I said. "More now than before."

"What else has occurred to you?"

"There's a slight chance Simms may be innocent."

"If she's innocent, who's guilty?"

"I love a good mystery, don't you?"

"Not that much," Lawrence said. "I like to read the last page of a mystery first."

"What's the Bureau going to do?" I said.

"Play Switzerland," Lawrence said. "Observe and stay neutral. For now."

"You have a take on things?"

"Off the record?"

"What am I, a reporter now?" I said.

"No, but I have a price."

"For your opinion?" I said. "Let me guess, two dozen."

"For checking seven hundred names?"

"I already paid for that."

"Call it a tip."

"Three dozen?"

"Deal. I'll expect them tomorrow afternoon."

"Fine."

"Assorted?"

"Fine, now would you please come on."

"My take on this is, somebody is targeting middle-aged women or not, or somebody is targeting orphans or not," Lawrence said.

"You went to college for that?"

"Don't forget to make it a nice selection," Lawrence said. "Not too many of any one thing."

"You want a stripper to deliver them?" I said. "A donut-gram?"

"This is Washington," Lawrence said. "We frown on such immorality."

I hung up, set the cell phone on the card table and placed the spent tube beside it.

Targeting middle-aged women, or not.

Targeting orphans, or not.

Otherwise known as the Potomac two-step.

Or not.

Say a lie often enough, people start to believe it.

When the people start to believe it, so do you.

When you start to believe it, it becomes true.

When it becomes true, unnamed sources quote it.

When it's quoted often enough, the lie becomes fact.

When it becomes fact, someone else will take credit for it.

The Potomac two-step.

A thought occurred to me.

What if somebody was targeting both?

CHAPTER 43

"It comes down to whom, if not Simms," Clark said after I told him about the new development. "And why? And when? And where? And is it simply coincidence about the others and completely unrelated to our case? Would a judge allow us to use the other murders as circumstantial evidence in court and if so, to what end? Others being murdered in similar fashion doesn't make Simms innocent of the murder she's on trial for."

"No, but a shred of doubt might," I said. "Imagine you're on the jury and it's been leaked that she passed her poly. Now imagine it's come out there were other men from the same home, all of them friends, murdered the same way, some of them found with middle-aged, cougar-type women. How would you vote?"

Clark stared at me.

"If I was on that jury and I knew Simms passed a poly and there were other men from the orphanage murdered in a similar fashion and my lawyer raised the question, could Simms possibly have been an intended victim as well, I would vote for a mistrial or at least a not guilty," I said.

"So would I," Clark said. "But I'm not going to be on the jury and neither will you."

"Maybe we can't prove Simms didn't kill Hughes at this point, but we can prove she didn't kill the others," I said. "Once the story breaks that former residents of Sacred Heart are dropping like flies, it all gets very muddled."

"And who will break that story?" Clark said.

"You will as part of a press conference," I said. "The usual 'in the course of my investigation defending my client, a string of similar crimes has come to light' song and dance."

Clark nodded as he mulled that over.

"The leak on the polygraph breaks when, tomorrow?" I said.

"Under the circumstances of this new information, I think it's to our advantage to have the leak break as close to jury selection as possible," Clark said. "Like an October surprise during an election."

"I agree," I said. "And that gives me time to check out the other three names."

"I want details on Sutton and . . . ?"

"Maggio," I said. "I'll have Paul Lawrence fax you his reports."

Clark looked at me for a moment.

"One regret I'll always have, Bekker, is that when we locked horns a decade ago we never got to finish that game," he said. "It would have been interesting to see who came out on top."

"Everything happened the way it was supposed to," I said. "Isn't that how it goes?"

"Maybe."

"I'll stop back in a few days," I said. "Maybe I'll have some new insight when I return from my trip."

I left Clark's office and went down to the street. City heat rose up from the pavement. I wasn't wearing a tie, but the suit jacket immediately stuck to my back. It wasn't quite air conditioning in the car weather yet, but it was coming fast.

I crossed the street and walked toward the lot where I left the Marquis.

Nothing much was going on. It was pre-lunch and the pedestrian traffic was light. There was no visible or viable reason the hairs on the back of my neck should stand up, but they did.

Something creeped me out and put me on full alert as I made my way to the other side of the street.

I paused in front of a storefront window to dig out the charger and remove a tube. As I placed the tube in my mouth, I used the window to do a quick scan of the street behind me.

Nothing was unusual or out of place.

On the surface.

I did a slow turn to take in the sidewalk and traffic, saw nothing to get in a twist about and started walking toward the lot. Then I saw it. A man on a bike between two cars at a red light. He was early twenties, muscular in his spandex riding gear, a black helmet covering his head.

He didn't so much look at me as try to avoid looking at me.

The lot was two blocks away. I took the long route and walked slowly.

Stay a cop long enough and you find there's no magic to things. If you think the husband did it, most times you'll be proven right. Think the kid on the bike is a threat of some kind, he will be.

I ducked into a Korean deli and bought a quart of orange juice so I could watch the street for a minute. The kid on the bike rode past the deli.

I left the deli with the orange juice in a paper bag, walked around the block, and stopped on the corner. Down the street at the intersection, the kid rode by with traffic.

I went around the block again and ducked into the street-level parking lot where I parked the Marquis. I stopped by the booth, gave the ticket and cash to the attendant on duty, retrieved the keys, walked ten rows deep and sat in my car with the engine running.

After about three minutes, the kid rode by the front entrance of the lot and slowed to a stop. He stayed on the bike, but his eyes scanned the lot until they settled on the Marquis.

I shoved the car into drive and gunned the gas.

The sudden movement jerked the kid and he took off pedaling.

I came out of the lot and made a right onto the street where I spotted the kid making a right turn at the corner.

I went up quick, made a right and picked him up a block ahead.

Traffic was just heavy enough to slow me down. The kid darted between cars and opened the lead, then made a sudden right turn.

By the time I reached the corner and made the turn, he was gone.

Like I said, there's no magic to being a cop.

The magic is being a cop long enough and staying alive.

CHAPTER 44

Walt said, "You're sure this wasn't just a kid taking a bike ride?"

I looked at Walt. We were in his office at the precinct.

"Okay, okay, I'll see who wants some overtime on special detail," Walt said.

"Two men who know what they're doing," I said. "No rookies fresh out of the box."

"How long?"

"Two days," I said. "I shouldn't be gone any longer than that."

"Then what?"

"Then I'll feel better."

"Heaven forbid," Walt said. "I wouldn't want you to feel bad."

"Call me later when you have a team."

I drove from the station house directly to Hope Springs Eternal, where I told Father Tomas it was essential Regan come stay with Janet for a few days while I was away on business.

The priest looked at me.

He didn't ask questions.

We've been down this road before.

I drove Regan, Sister Mary Martin and Molly the cat to Janet's house in the suburbs.

Janet was on the midnight shift and taking a quick nap while Mark was at school.

To her credit, she didn't panic when I told her there was a possibility I was being watched and thought it best for all if

Regan, along with a team of cops, stayed with her for a few days.

We had coffee in the kitchen with Sister Mary Martin while Regan put her stuff away in the spare bedroom.

Molly rubbed my leg.

"Why can't you just not go on your trip?" Janet said.

"Couple of reasons," I said. "One is I'm not a hundred percent sure I'm being watched and this is just a precaution. Two is if I'm right, I'd rather have things in place sooner than later. Three is I want to end this thing as quickly as possible and to do that, I need more information. Four, I trust Walt to protect all of you with his life if necessary."

"That's more than a couple," Janet said.

"Mr. Bekker, this is the second time we've had to do something like this in six months because of your work," Sister Mary Martin said. "I hope this isn't the norm for you because Regan needs a stable environment if she is to live with you on a permanent basis."

"After this, I'm retired," I said. "I gave my word and I won't break it."

Janet looked at me.

"I've asked Janet to marry me and I think she said yes," I said. "However, since I'm a man and not that smart, I'm not really sure."

Sister Mary Martin looked at Janet.

Janet nodded at the nun. "If he doesn't get himself killed first," she said.

"A lot of freezing sinners in hell right now," Sister Mary Martin said.

We both looked at the nun.

"I'll go give Regan a hand," Sister Mary Martin said.

She left the table and Molly followed her out of the kitchen.

I pulled out my cell phone as I stood up and walked to the

sliding kitchen doors. I took a chair at the patio table and called Jane. After several transfers, she came on the line.

"I'm at Janet's house," I said. "Remember where it is?"

"I do," Jane said.

"It's in your jurisdiction, isn't it?"

"It is."

"Whoever you have in a cruiser nearby, ask them to make a pass-by every thirty minutes," I said.

"Because?"

I gave her the short version.

"Becoming a habit with you, isn't it," Jane remarked.

"Need I remind you I took this job as a favor to you," I said.

"Ouch," Jane said. "Okay, I have four cars on tonight. I'll have them rotate a pass-by every thirty minutes."

"Thanks," I said. "It's just a precaution, but I don't like taking chances."

"Nuff said," Jane said.

I hung up and called Kagan at his office.

"Frank, Bekker," I said. "I'll fill you in later, but get over to Crist's and have the guards doubled and make sure they stay on patrol. Alert and awake. No sleeping in the guardhouse. Tell the ladies not to leave the grounds for any reason and if they insist, two men go with them. No arguments. No exceptions."

"Because?"

"There's a kid on a bike and I don't like him," I said.

"And that's code for what?" Kagan said.

"Do it," I said. "I'll give you the details later."

Not until I set the phone down did I feel Janet's stare.

"What?" I said.

"You're never so animated as when there's danger involved," Janet said.

"Danger is what I'm trying to prevent."

"It's just . . . I never see you come this alive when we're doing the ordinary," Janet said. "I'm thinking you might not be ready to quit and settle down. The ordinary is what marriage and life is all about, Jack. I'm not sure you understand that just yet."

"This isn't about that," I said. "There's something going on that shouldn't be and I don't know what it is. It could be nothing. It could be dangerous. I can't and won't risk you, Regan, Mark or anyone else until I'm sure that it's nothing. Once this is done and we settle down as a family, things will work out the way they should."

Janet stared at me.

Mark came home from school just then.

"I saw your car, Uncle Jack," he said as he tossed his backpack to the lawn.

"Regan's here, too," I said. "She'll be staying a few days while I'm away on business."

"Cool," Mark said. "She upstairs?"

"Second spare bedroom," Janet said.

Mark dashed back to the kitchen doors.

"Hey, no video games until homework is done," Janet called after him.

"Aw, Mom," Mark said as he went inside.

"You'll be trading in a gun and badge for homework, laundry detail and mowing the lawn," Janet said to me. "Will you be this animated when it's your turn to do the dishes?"

"I screwed up my first marriage and my daughter because of the gun and badge," I said. "I won't make that mistake again."

"You're sure?"

"Positive."

"Good," Janet said as she stood up. "Then you won't mind helping me with dinner. You can wash the lettuce."

CHAPTER 45

While Janet changed for work and Sister Mary Martin read a book in her bedroom, Mark, Regan and I played a video game in the living room. The game consisted of an alien predator on Earth hunting soldiers for sport. We took turns being the alien. Turns out, I'm lousy at video games. Turns out, Regan is a whiz and creamed the both of us four out of the five games we played. I suspected she let Mark win one when she winked at me as her alien creature fell to his barrage of bullets.

Mark fell asleep first. We were keeping him home from school tomorrow so he could sleep it off in the morning. Regan went next, close to eleven-thirty. She slept on Mark's shoulder like a big sister.

I shut down the video game and turned on the news.

Dressed in hospital whites, Janet came downstairs and sat beside me on the crowded sofa.

"What's this?" she said and nodded at the sleeping beauties.

"Overstimulation," I said.

"Like you get when you see the birthmark on my . . ."

"Video game stimulation," I said. "And as you can see, it has the opposite effect."

"I'm going to be late for work," Janet said.

"You're lucky I'm letting you go."

"Well, aren't we the silverback beating our chest."

The doorbell rang.

"That would be Walt and his men," I said.

I went to the door to let them in.

Walt said, "This is Detective Markel and Detective Cooper. They had excessive vacation time and took three days. They'll be your house guests."

Markel and Cooper were in their mid-thirties and had the look of seasoned, capable detectives.

Janet came to the door.

"This is the lady of the house," Walt said. "And the boss. Make no mistake about that."

Janet greeted Walt with a kiss on the cheek.

"I believe Bekker has lost what little mind he has left," she said.

"Who said he had any left?" Walt said.

"I'll show them around the house, then I have to go to work," Janet said.

The detectives followed Janet into the living room.

"I'm surprised you're letting her go to work," Walt said.

"She put her foot down and it's bigger than mine," I said. "One of your men can pick her up at eight."

"No problem," Walt said. "So, after reflection, how sure are you about this terrorist on a bike?"

"He played cat and mouse with me," I said. "I ditched him and hid in my car in the lot near Clark's. He knew my car and came to check it out. He took off when he spotted me and I lost him in traffic."

Walt looked at me. I knew what he was thinking. The bike kid knew my car and knew Clark's office. That meant the surveillance had been going on for a while. What else did the kid know?

And whatever the kid did know, who else knew?

"Somebody doesn't want you to find something out," Walt said. "Or thinks that you already did."

"Yeah, but about whom and what?" I said. "Simms, one of

the dead boys or one of the dead women?"

"Who's the target, John?" Walt said. "The murdered victims from the home or the middle-aged women?"

"What if the victims were the men and somebody used the women as decoys to lure them to the motel rooms?" I said.

"Why kill the women?" Walt said. "And why let some of them go?"

"I don't know."

"And that implies that Simms is part of some murder plot to kill orphaned men, and that makes no sense at all."

"No, it doesn't."

"Clark's office is in the city and that's my turf," Walt said. "That means I can now take an active part in this mess."

"What, you're going to put an APB out on a bike?" I said.

"Smartass, I'll tell you what I'm going to do," Walt said. "I'm going to put surveillance on Clark's office and the Crist mansion and maybe we'll get lucky and catch us a two-wheeled suspect."

Janet came up behind me.

"Bekker, if you ever expect to get lucky with me again, I suggest that you drive me to work," she said. "And by lucky I mean you know what I mean."

I did.

"We'll talk later," I told Walt.

We took the Marquis. The hospital was thirty minutes from Janet's home. The ride was silent. Not that Janet was angry with me, but she allowed me to drive and lose myself in my thoughts.

I'm sure she was doing the same.

Five minutes from the hospital, Janet broke her silence.

"Bekker, care to know what I think?" she said.

"Sure."

"I think, for the first time that maybe she didn't do it," Janet said. "The fact that somebody feels the need to follow you around means somebody else is involved. If somebody else is involved, maybe that somebody else is the guilty one?"

"I was thinking the same thing," I said. "Now all I have to do is prove it."

CHAPTER 46

The waxing moon was high overhead when I parked the Marquis in the lot after dropping Janet off. I walked along the connector to the beach. The sand was illuminated just enough to see across the beach to the dark ocean. I could hear but not see waves crashing at high tide.

Even from the half-mile distance to my trailer and Oz's, I could see the lights on in both of them. Oz rarely stayed up past midnight. I didn't leave any lights on. I broke into a jog that ended in a sprint at Oz's trailer. I pulled the .45 from the small of my back as I ran.

Between the moon and the lights, it was bright enough for me to see the bicycle tire tracks in the sand.

Oz's door was open.

I burst into the trailer with the .45 in my right hand.

Oz wasn't there.

I came out and looked five hundred feet down the beach to my trailer. I hadn't left a light on when I left this morning because I planned to be back early enough to have dinner with Oz.

I sprinted to my trailer.

Oz was face down in front of my open trailer door.

The bike was nowhere to be seen, but the tracks in the sand were visible all around my trailer.

I knelt down beside Oz. He was unconscious. Thankfully, he was still breathing. I rolled him over. His face was a bloody pulp. So now I knew the kid on the bike wasn't harmless.

I pulled out my cell phone and dialed 911.

I did a quick check of my trailer while I waited for the ambulance to arrive. Nothing appeared disturbed. I moved the kitchen table and pulled up the trap door. In the pit, the semi-auto shotgun, a gift from Crist, was still in place.

I called Walt with the news.

"A guy doesn't get much sleep hanging around with you," he said, but agreed to meet me at the hospital where Janet was on duty.

Oz didn't wake up when the EMTs put him in the ambulance. I asked them if he could be taken to Janet's hospital instead of the city dump they usually transport 911 victims to.

Forty-five minutes later, Walt met me in the emergency room waiting area.

"How is he?" Walt said.

"Don't know yet."

"Janet know you're here?"

"I saw her for a second," I said. "She's in with him and the doctors."

"The fucking kid on the bike?" Walt said.

"Bike tracks all over the place," I said.

"Was he looking for something in particular?"

"Me."

"Any chance you could recognize him?"

"None."

"So the advantage is to him."

"Us," I said. "He's tipped his hand before the dealer turned over the final card. A pro would have waited until he was sure I had something conclusive."

"Unless he just wanted you out of the way," Walt suggested.

"Why?"

"We both know why," Walt said. "You're getting too close to

something and he wants to keep that something from going public."

"Like?"

"We both know that one, too," Walt said. "Evidence that Simms may be innocent. An innocent Simms means a guilty someone else. That stands to reason."

"Except that everything I've learned so far makes her appear even guiltier."

"Bike guy doesn't know that," Walt said. "Bike guy doesn't want to take that chance."

"Bike guy came to my trailer to kill me," I said. "That means he's desperate. That means he'll try again, if not me, then Clark, or maybe both of us."

"I'll speak to my men and have them on alert," Walt said. "Nothing's going to happen, John. Don't worry."

"It already happened, Walt," I said. "I covered all the bases except one."

Janet came into the waiting area. Walt and I stood up.

"Oz has four broken ribs, a broken nose, a separated shoulder and blood in his lungs," Janet said. "Another hour and he wouldn't have made it. He would have drowned in his own blood."

"But he made it?" I said.

Janet nodded. "Thankfully, yes."

"Where is he?" I said.

"He's in recovery," Janet said. "Probably until morning. The doctors told me he should recover fully within six weeks, although he can probably go home in two."

"Can I see him?" I said.

"Just for a minute."

Janet led Walt and me down a long hallway to a recovery room in the emergency ward. She entered and clicked on a light. Oz's face was covered in a white bandage. His shoulder was in a harness. Tubes connected to IV bottles were inserted in his arms. A monitor blipped out his vital signs.

Janet went to the bed.

Walt and I stayed in the background.

"Oz?" she said softly. "Company."

Slowly, Oz opened his eyes.

"Am I dead?" he rasped.

Janet smiled. "No."

"Good, 'cause I'd hate to think I quit drinking and went to heaven and got to look at those two ugly mugs behind you for eternity," Oz said.

Janet looked at me.

"You got that right, Oz," she said. "An uglier pair of mutts I've never seen."

I stood beside Janet.

"Oz, tell me what happened," I said.

"Got up to use the bathroom," Oz said. "Saw a light on in your trailer. I thought it was you. I walked down to tell you a man knocked on my door looking for you earlier."

"What man?"

"Young, maybe twenty-five," Oz said. "Said he had a message for you. That was around five in the afternoon. I told him you weren't home and he could leave the message with me. He said he'd come back later. Then he left."

"What did he look like?" I said.

"Tall. Dark hair and eyes. Had on that outfit bike riders wear."

"Spandex?"

"Yeah."

"So you went to my trailer and what happened?"

"I never saw him," Oz said. "I never saw a thing. Next thing I know, I'm in this bed wired like the inside of an old TV set."

"That's enough for now," Janet said. "He needs to rest."

"I'll stop by tomorrow, Oz," I said.

"Hey, Bekker," Oz said. "Being your friend is no picnic."

"Try being his girlfriend," Janet said with a sneer.

I kissed Janet goodbye in the hallway and walked outside with Walt. We stood in the hospital parking lot. I stuck a vapor tube between my lips.

"He could have killed Oz," I said.

"Oz wasn't his target," Walt said. "Oz was just in the way. And that piece of plastic you're sucking on looks about as inviting as toothpaste on stale white bread."

"I'm not liking bike guy much," I said. "And like caviar, this piece of plastic is an acquired taste."

"Let me know when they start selling caviar in one-ounce plastic tubes."

I blew a vapor smoke ring.

"Tomorrow, I'll have a sketch artist work with Oz," Walt said. "We may get lucky on a sketch. In the meantime, you watch your fucking ass."

Watch your fucking ass.

Good advice.

So was always carry an umbrella on a cloudy day.

I didn't have much use for either.

CHAPTER 47

"Somebody doesn't want the results of her poly revealed," Clark said when I called him from the airport early the next morning.

"Could be, but I'm not sure," I said. "Somebody would have to have leaked it to bike boy or whoever he's working for in order for there to be a leak from our side."

"So what else could it be?" Clark said.

"Simms is innocent and the murderer or murderers want to keep her guilty," I said. "A guilty Simms is an innocent them."

"That makes sense, doesn't it?"

"You know what else makes sense, you get a private body-guard."

"Not to worry," Clark said. "I have plenty of mob buddies who have a keen interest in seeing me live."

"Does it make sense Simms was the target and Hughes just happened to get in the way?" I said.

"No," Clark said. "But that doesn't mean it isn't so."

"I got to catch my plane," I said. "I'll call you from Austin."

"Watch your ass, Bekker," Clark said.

"And I've got an umbrella, too," I said.

"What the fuck does that mean?" Clark said.

"Call you later," I said and hung up.

The last time I was in Austin, Texas, it was a medium-size, cowboy town known for amateur music and rustic scenery. That was twenty years ago for a police training conference. I stayed at the Doral, a cowboy hotel built in 1885.

I stayed there again in a balcony room that overlooked the main drag and the dome of the state capital.

After checking in, I went for a walk.

Austin had grown. A lot. It was a large, modern and very safe city. The area was now a haven for filmmakers, music, art and the computer industry. Still, the cowboy flair was present on every street and the smell of Mexican food cooking carried from block to block.

I found the small art gallery and frame shop operated by Michael Votto eleven blocks from my hotel. It had a great view of the state capital building. The dome gleamed in the sunlight.

When I entered the shop, a tiny bell mounted on the door announced my presence.

Michael Votto came out from a back room. He wasn't quite a modern-day hippie, but he was close. Long dark ponytail, a full dark beard, rimless glasses. He wiped a thin paintbrush with a rag as he stood behind the counter and looked at me.

"Help you, man?" Votto said.

"Are you Michael Votto?"

"I am. Who are you?"

I removed my ID and set it on the counter. Votto gave it a quick, cursory onceover.

"I work for an attorney representing Carly Simms in the murder of Jon Hughes," I said. "If you can spare a few minutes, I'd like to talk to you."

"I figured somebody would show up," Votto said. "I talked with Joey a few days ago. He saw it on the news and told me Jon was dead. It came as a shock somebody would kill him like that. Do you know why she did it?"

"No, do you?"

Votto stared at me from behind his glasses, then shook his head. "Was a joke, right?"

"I wish it were," I said. "So, can we talk for a few minutes about Jon Hughes?"

"Sure," Votto said. "But can we do it out back? I'm kind of in the middle of something."

I followed Votto to a large back room that was filled with frames and paintings, tables loaded with tools, cans, paint and other items I wasn't familiar enough with to name. A door secured with a padlock could have led to a backyard, but I doubted that. A crease of light escaped from a thin sliver at the bottom of the door. Votto stopped at a table where a large frame sat on a brace and started rubbing it with a tiny brush.

"Frame is two hundred years old," Votto said. "I'm restoring it for a gallery uptown."

"Great," I said. "So what can you tell me about Hughes?"

Votto shook his head. "Ain't seen him in six years," he said. "Since I got out and moved to Austin to study art. Austin is a mecca for art, you know."

"I know," I said. "Talk to him much?"

"Never."

"But you talk to Joseph Buck?"

"Once in a while," Votto said. "I painted a logo for his plane, a Cessna 182. He called me about Jon after seeing the story on the news."

"Did you like Jon?"

"Sure, well enough."

"Just not well enough to keep in touch."

"Nothing to keep in touch about," Votto said. "He was into computers. I'm into art. Not much to relate to other than being raised in a home by strangers."

"What time you close up shop?" I said.

"Around five, but I usually don't get out of here before six. Why?"

"I thought maybe we could have dinner and you can tell me what it's like to grow up in a home."

"Can't," Votto said. "Got plans. I can tell you what it's like to grow up in a home, though. It sucks. A lot."

I nodded.

"I'm at the Doral if you remember anything or change your mind."

"I won't and I won't," Votto said. "Like I said, I haven't seen Jon since the day I left Sacred Heart. Sorry, man, that's all I can tell you."

"Sure."

I walked back to the hotel and had some lunch at a sidewalk café. I stopped by the desk on the way in and told the clerk to give me a call at four. Then I went to my room and took a nap.

I woke up fifteen minutes before the wakeup call and grabbed a quick shower. I left the hotel wearing slacks and a short-sleeve shirt and arrived at Votto's shop at ten of five.

The little bell rang when I opened the door and he came out from the back room. He recognized me immediately and stopped behind the counter as if to create a barrier.

"I already told you everything I know," Votto said.

"I don't think so," I said. "I think you're a liar."

"I don't care what you think," Votto said.

"Maybe the police will care about the pot factory you've got growing in the locked closet in the back room," I said.

Votto stared at me.

I stared at him.

"Suit yourself," I said and whipped out my cell phone.

"I have glaucoma," Votto said. "Severe. It's the only thing that eliminates the pain and eases the pressure in my eyes."

"What's that number for the police again?" I said. "Oh, yes. 911."

"If they allowed it for medical use around here, I wouldn't have to grow it," Votto said. "Man, my doctor told me to grow it. I can have him . . ."

193

"You can talk to the police or you can have a nice, quiet meal and talk to me," I said. "Do you like Mexican? I saw a place looked good a few blocks from here."

Votto stared at me.

"What's it going to be?" I said.

"Mexican's good," Votto said.

CHAPTER 48

"So how bad are your eyes that you'd risk jail?" I said.

Votto took a sip of strong Mexican coffee. He set the cup down and removed his glasses so I could get a good look.

"Sometimes the pressure is so bad, I just want to hide under the covers and cry," he said. "The marijuana is the only thing I've tried that eliminates the pain. The doctor tells me I've got maybe ten good years left before I need to invest in a dog. Know what it feels like to lose something you love doing?"

"Yes, I do," I said. "I know exactly how that feels."

The waiter at Juan's Authentic Mexican brought us our meals.

"So what do you want to ask me about?" Votto said as he replaced his glasses.

"You grew up in the home with Jon Hughes, Scott Lind, Thomas Sutton and Robert Maggio," I said. "What can you tell me about them?"

"Jon was an okay guy, I guess," Votto said. "Liked karate, played with computers. Scott was into football. Sutton and Maggio, I don't remember much. They were older, I think. It wasn't like we were the only ones there. Half the guys there I never even knew their names."

"What about girls?" I said.

"Weren't any," Votto said.

"I know that," I said. "But did you talk about them? Teenage boys, all those hormones, you guys must have talked about girls."

"Sure, all the time," Votto said.

"What kinds of girls was Hughes interested in?" I said.

"I'm not following you. Interested how?"

"Hughes, Lind, Sutton and Maggio were all killed in motel rooms with women twenty years older than them," I said. "It's a pattern."

"Oh," Votto said. "You want to know if they had a cougar/milf thing going?"

"The pattern does suggest that," I said.

"We weren't even exposed to girls our own age, much less older women," Votto said. "If they had a thing going for cougars, I wasn't aware of it. Maybe it developed later when they got out?"

"What about you?"

"My girlfriend's twenty-three, want to talk to her?"

"No. What about enemies? Someone at the home who didn't get along with them, maybe fought with them, anything like that?"

"Guys used to fight like cats and dogs all the time about anything," Votto said. "Teenage guys locked up, what do you expect?"

"Someone with enough resentment to carry a grudge and act upon it on the outside," I said.

Votto sipped his coffee after taking a bite of razor-thin sliced beef.

"That Ty Butler was a real whack job," he said. "Did you talk to him?"

"If Butler has any involvement, he's doing it from state prison in Ohio," I said.

"Doesn't surprise me one bit."

"What about Stousser and Buck?"

"Stephen always had his face in a book and all Joey talked about was becoming a pilot," Votto said. "I'd like to tell you more, but I really don't know more. I'm sorry those guys are dead and I wish I could help you find whoever did it, but it's all I know. If it's not enough to suit you, I'm sorry, but that's all I got."

"I found out what I came for," I said.

"What's that?" Votto said.

"You're innocent," I said.

After parting ways with Votto, I returned to my hotel and called Janet.

"Oz is recovering well and should be released in a few days into my custody," she said. "I made arrangements for a hospital bed to be delivered to my house so I can take care of him for a few weeks or so until he's strong enough. He's a tough old bird, I'll give him that."

"Walt's men?"

"In the way, but no real problem."

"And how are you holding up?" I said.

"Against my better judgment, I'll inflate your ego and tell you I miss you terribly."

"My ego has a permanent hole in it so it never gets inflated," I said. "Regan and Mark?"

"Right now they're in the fifth inning of video baseball," Janet said. She paused, then said, "Living away from the hospital seems to suit her, Jack. She's come a long way in a short time since you're back in her life."

"I know."

"We're doing the right thing."

"I know."

"So you'll be home when?"

"My flight from Denver lands around one in the morning tomorrow."

"I'll be at work."

"I'll stop by on my way home."

"Bring me flowers," Janet said. "You owe me that much."

I hung up thinking I owed her a great deal more than that.

CHAPTER 49

Joseph Buck was tooling around with the engine of his Cessna 182 plane when I arrived at the private airstrip twenty minutes west of Denver. I parked the rental car and entered the hangar.

"Yeah, Mike said you might show up here," Buck said after I showed him my ID. "He said it was cool to talk to you, that you weren't looking to fuck anybody over."

"I'm not," I said. "Unless finding the guilty is considered fucking someone over, all I'm after is facts and truth."

Buck stared at me.

"Just want you to know where I stand," I said.

Buck closed the hood on the Cessna and wiped his hands on a rag. He was around six feet tall, medium build, sandy hair and blue eyes. He had the kind of face that always appeared to be smiling, even when he wasn't.

He tossed the rag onto a worktable. "So what do you think of my plane?"

I gave the Cessna 182 a quick onceover. "Yours?"

"It will be in about fifteen years," Buck said. "It's ten years old, but Cessnas are good for forty years or more. This one tops out at two hundred miles an hour and the landing gear is retractable, so there's less drag and better mileage."

"What do you plan to do with it?" I said.

"Charters," Buck said. "Corporate gigs, special deliveries, county rescue and anything else comes my way."

"How long have you had your license?" I said.

"Eighteen months," Buck said. "I was just going to do some takeoffs and landings. Want to join me? We can talk while I practice."

"Why not."

I sat beside Buck while he taxied onto the runway. It didn't take much and we were in the air. We climbed and leveled out at seventy-five miles an hour.

"Hey, you ain't mad at Mike for calling me?" Buck said.

"I didn't tell him not to," I said. "And I figured he would."

"He designed the logo I'm going to use once my charter license is approved."

"He told me."

Buck nodded as he eased us into a turn and climbed another two hundred feet.

"So what do you want to know?" he said.

"Who killed Jon Hughes," I said.

Buck cocked his head at me. "That woman like the news said. Hold on."

He took us into a hairpin turn that left my stomach two feet behind me.

"I don't think so," I said. "I think that . . ."

"Hold on," Buck said again.

We came out of the turn and dipped three hundred feet. Below me, I could feel the landing gear descend. I held onto my stomach as Buck guided us into a feather-like landing on the runway.

"What were you saying?" Buck said.

"I said, I think someone from the home might have a major beef with you guys," I said. "Enough of a beef they want to kill you all and are using women as a possible lure to get you alone."

Buck stared at me for a moment.

"That Butler is crazy," he said. "Mike said you told him he's doing time, so I guess it ain't him."

"Anybody else?"

"Who'd want to kill Jon?"

"Or you."

"What the fuck have I done?" Buck said, suddenly animated. "Growing up in the home was hard, man. I won't lie to you. Every moment sucked and I'll tell you why. Because nobody wanted us. We're supposed to be guys and not care we don't have mommy's love, but that's all bullshit. Every last kid in there is fucked up and scarred for life, but to kill over it like that is a completely different level of fucked up. That's just my opinion."

"So who is fucked up on a different level?" I said.

"Hey, you're the cop," Buck said. "So, I'm gonna do some more practice runs. Wanna go?"

"No thanks," I said and got out.

I found out what I came for.

I returned to the airport, where I had a four-hour wait for my flight to Minneapolis.

I called Walt on my cell phone.

"Where are you?" he said.

"Denver, on my way to Minneapolis."

"To see that Stousser kid?"

"Yeah."

"Don't bother," Walt said. "I just read a report on the wire from the Minneapolis PD that says they found him in his dorm room. Somebody broke his neck like a chicken bone about twelve hours ago."

"Stephen Stousser, you're sure?"

"I've been doing some hunting and pecking on my own," Walt said. "I talked to Minneapolis last night and asked for a bio on the kid. They got back to me this morning with the report. I was just about to track you down."

"What about Michael Votto?" I said. "I talked to him last night."

"He's alive as far as I know," Walt said.

"Check and call me back right away," I said.

I grabbed another rental and sped back to the private airport. Joseph Buck was in the air when I screeched to a stop in front of his hangar. I smoked a vapor tube while I watched him come in for another feather-like landing. I had to admit, the kid knew his way behind the controls.

I walked out on the runway and waved my arms.

Buck turned off the engine, opened his door and jumped down to the pavement. He walked toward me. I met him in the middle of the runway.

"Stousser is dead," I said. "Murdered in his dorm room last night."

"What?" Buck said, his face immediately draining of all color.

"Let's go in the office," I said.

We entered the hangar and opened the door to the small adjacent office, where Buck flopped into a chair at the desk.

"How?" he said.

"Somebody broke his neck in his door room last night," I said. "Somebody might come to break yours today."

"Why? I haven't done a goddamn thing to anybody."

"They think you know something."

"What the fuck do I know?" Buck said. "I know how to fly single-engine planes, that's what I know. I got nothing to do with any of this shit, whatever this shit is. You gotta believe me."

Buck was genuinely scared right down to his socks.

"What about Stousser, what does he know?" I said.

"Fuck, man, I haven't seen the guy since I moved to Denver," Buck said. "Even Mike, he did the work for him online based on digital photos. How do I know what this fucking crazy guy thinks we know?"

"Listen, Joseph, I need you to calm down and stay focused," I said.

"Fuck me, man," Buck said. "Three years of working shit jobs to get my license and for what? So some asshole from the home can fucking kill me for some shit I don't even know or care about. Fuck me, man."

I slapped Buck across the face. His head snapped back and he nearly fell from the chair. I waited for the bell in his head to stop ringing and he looked at me. My hand print glowed on his right cheek.

"I'll make sure the PD in Denver knows what's going on," I said. "Where do you live?"

"Fifteen minutes from here."

"I'll follow you."

"My plane."

"Put it away," I said. "I'll wait."

While Buck taxied his plane into the hangar, Walt called me back with an update.

"So far the Votto kid's okay," Walt said. "I asked Austin PD to check him out and give him a heads-up. They said they would keep an eye on him, but they can't babysit him around the clock. What do you think?"

"I think Simms didn't kill Jon Hughes," I said. "I think someone from Sacred Heart has a major beef and is getting revenge on these guys years later."

"Why wait five or six years?" Walt said. "What's the point or the benefit in waiting?"

"He's got a reason, Walt," I said. "I don't know what it is, but it's there. Any news on the bike rider?"

"Nothing," Walt said. "Kid probably skipped or is laying low after his little tap dance on Oz."

"Shit," I said.

"What?"

"I forgot about that kid Josh Andrus in Utah," I said.

"I'll call the state police and ask them to do a check on him," Walt said.

"I got his work number," I said. "I'll call him there."

"Ring me back in thirty minutes," Walt said.

I was searching the numbers file in my phone when Buck entered the office.

"Plane's put away," he said. "Now what?"

"Now you wait while I make a call," I said and dialed the number for the security desk at the TRAX Corporation.

"Security," a male voice said.

"Josh Andrus, please," I said. "This is John Bekker calling."

"Sorry, sir, Josh isn't here right now."

"Put me through to Sal Meeks," I said. "This is urgent."

"Hold."

I held.

Sal Meeks came on the line and said, "Mr. Bekker, what can I do for you?"

"Josh Andrus," I said. "I need to speak with him right away."

"Oh, I'm afraid he won't be in for several more days," Meeks said. "He injured his shoulder at a karate tournament last week and needed some time off. He's taking sick days."

"Do you have his home number?" I said. "It's really important."

Meeks gave me the number. I punched it in and after three rings, Josh picked up the phone.

"Josh, John Bekker," I said. "I need to talk to you."

"Hi, Mr. Bekker," Josh said. "How are you?"

"Fine, how's the shoulder?" I said. "Sal Meeks told me you injured it."

"Yeah, I slipped on the mat during a takedown," Josh said. "It's not a serious injury. I just can't use it is all. A few days' rest and I'll be fine."

"Good," I said. "Josh, listen carefully. I have good reason to believe someone from Sacred Heart is targeting former residents who were there during the time you were. I just received word that Stephen Stousser was murdered in his dorm room last night. Along with Scott Lind, Thomas Sutton and Robert Maggio, it's too much of a coincidence to think otherwise."

"I haven't done anything," Josh said. "To anybody," he added.

"That doesn't matter right now," I said. "What does matter is that you protect yourself. Don't open your door unless you know who it is. Don't go out alone and keep your eyes open when you do go out. If you see someone following you on a bike, that could be our man."

"On a bike?"

"Someone on a bike followed me and beat up a friend pretty bad when I wasn't home," I said.

"Jeez," Josh said. "Around here, everyone is on a bike."

"Just be careful," I said. "I'll have the PD alerted to the situation, but just be careful and keep your eyes open and your door locked all the time."

"Sure, Mr. Bekker," Josh said. "I will."

"Still have my number?"

"I do."

"Call me if you see anything suspicious," I said. "Right after you call 911."

"I will, but don't worry, Mr. Bekker. I'm not exactly helpless."

"Josh, his weapon is the element of surprise," I said. "The edge is to him. Understand?"

"Sure."

"I'll check back with you later."

I stuck my phone in a pocket and looked at Buck.

"Josh Andrus?" Buck said.

I nodded.

"Let's go," I said.
"Where?"
"Your place."

Chapter 50

Joseph Buck lived in a low-income housing complex that was set back in the woods just far enough so that the road wasn't visible from Buck's windows. Thirty two-story buildings were surrounded by a brown fence with access through a gate operated by a card key.

Buck lived in a one-bedroom apartment on the second floor of building number twenty-one. It was standard low-income fare, with a lone bedroom, a kitchen, living room, and bathroom. Laundry was done in the basement machines. Buck's furniture was inexpensive, but well kept and clean.

"Got any coffee?" I said.

"Yeah."

"Make some."

I sat on the sofa and pulled out my cell phone.

Buck went to the kitchen to make the coffee.

I called Walt.

"I talked to the Utah State Police and gave them a heads-up," Walt said. "I don't see what more we can do at this point except wait for something to break."

"I called the Andrus kid at home," I said. "He's got an injured shoulder from a karate match, but he's a smart kid. I think he'll be all right."

"Where are you?"

"Joseph Buck's apartment," I said. "Kid's scared and he has a right to be. Half the kids he grew up with have been murdered and he doesn't want to be next."

"When you coming home?"

"Tonight. I should be in by nine. Do me a favor and call Clark and let him know what's going on," I said.

"I don't even know what's going on, but I'll call him," Walt said.

"Walt, I don't need to ask this, but . . ."

"Then don't ask," Walt said. "I'll be at Janet's until you get there."

"Thanks."

"Screw off," Walt said.

I replaced the phone.

"Coffee's ready," Buck said from the kitchen.

I joined him at the small table.

"So, I'm okay, right?" Buck said.

"You heard what I told Josh?"

"Yeah."

"Same rules apply to you," I said.

Buck nodded.

"I've been thinking about Sacred Heart," Buck said. "Do you know why I was there?"

I took a sip of coffee from an oversized mug and shook my head. "No."

"My parents died in a car wreck when I was just six," Buck said. "That was in Idaho. I bounced around from family member to family member until I was eight or nine. I wound up moving to Utah to live with my aunt and uncle. Uncle had a hobby. He liked to fondle little boys when Auntie wasn't home. One day she was. The state sent me to Sacred Heart. As horrible as it is to have no family when you're a kid, they did a good job taking care of me. I have no beef with them. Or anybody."

"Somebody has a beef with somebody," I said. "Until that

somebody is caught, I think it best if you stayed someplace else for a while and didn't tell anybody where that place is."

"I got no place else," Buck said. "I can barely pay the rent on this place, the mortgage on the Cessna is so high."

"What if you stayed at the airport for a while?" I suggested. "Set up shop in the hangar with your plane. They have airport security and when it's locked down, no one is getting in or out."

"That's not a bad idea," Buck said.

"Take down my cell number," I said. "Call me anytime."

"Maybe I should buy a gun?"

"Do you know how to use a gun?"

"No."

"Buy some pepper spray instead," I said. "At least you can't shoot yourself in the foot with it."

There wasn't much else I could do besides move in with him, so I left Joseph Buck at his table and returned to the airport. Two hours later, I was on a flight home. The sick feeling in my gut wasn't caused by the landing.

CHAPTER 51

Sister Mary Martin, Regan, Mark and two detectives were watching a thirty-five-year-old rerun of *Little House on the Prairie* when I arrived at Janet's house from the airport.

Oz was asleep or sedated in the hospital bed beside the sofa.

"Janet's been called in to work an emergency shift," Sister Mary Martin said.

"I'll sleep on the sofa tonight," I said.

"Are you hungry?"

"I could eat."

"I'll throw something together," Sister Mary Martin said.

"How was your trip?" Mark asked me as I sat between him and Regan.

"Tiresome," I said.

"Your friend was here," Mark said.

"Walt?"

Mark nodded.

"He had to go, but he said he would be back in a little while to stay with us."

"He say why he had to leave?"

Mark shook his head.

"I'll find out when he comes back."

I looked at Regan.

To me, the only word she'd spoken was to call me Dad and even that happened just a few times. I knew that she spoke with Sister Mary Martin in private and that was okay with me. There was a decade-long trust built upon mutual love and understanding.

I realized that what I had done to my daughter was not unlike what the hundreds of boys experienced at Sacred Heart. I abandoned her when she needed me most. I wasn't strong enough to take the pain of losing my wife and crawled inside a bottle for a decade while my daughter suffered the most.

How do you make that up to your daughter?

How do you give her back the years you've both lost?

Press reset and start over?

Hit delete.

I had no idea.

"Uncle Jack, are you crying?" Mark said.

"I need some air," I said.

I went to the kitchen, slid open the doors and sat at the backyard patio table. I was alone for a few minutes and then Regan was in the chair beside me.

"Dad?" she said in her little girl's voice.

Her hand was out.

I took it in mine.

We sat there in the dark holding hands.

It was the best moment I've had in thirteen years.

Maybe my whole stupid life.

CHAPTER 52

I was the only one awake when Walt picked me up at seven the next morning. He had two coffee containers in a paper bag. I grabbed one and gave him the other.

"You told Jane you want another look at the motel room?" Walt said.

"She'll meet us there."

"What do you expect to find this time?"

"Third time's a charm," I said.

"So is extra sleep."

I grinned and took a sip of coffee.

"Something's bugging me and I don't know what that is," I said.

"Besides four unexplained murders involving kids from the same orphanage, a state prosecutor charged with murder in the first degree, a kid on a bike beating up old men, no evidence and no clues, what could possibly be bugging you?" Walt said.

I sipped coffee and shook my head.

"Want to know what I think?" Walt said.

"No."

"I think what's bugging you is that you think Simms is innocent and you have no way of proving it."

I looked at Walt.

"I feel the same way," Walt said.

We met Jane for breakfast at the diner near the Peek A Boo Motel.

"You have the files I asked for?" I asked Jane.

"In the cruiser," Jane said. "I figured we could have breakfast in peace so I don't get indigestion."

"How's the morning sickness?" I said.

Walt looked at Jane. "What, again? What's that make, like eleven, twelve?"

"My husband is a selfish prick," Jane said. "Excuse the pun."

"Anything on a cab?" I said.

"No one has come forward yet to say they picked them up," Jane said. "Same for the .32 and laptop. Oh, there were dust particles in Hughes's hair. Small traces from the air vent like you thought."

"And that means what?" Walt said.

"He fell asleep or passed out," I said. "Which can account for the long period of time between when they arrived and when he was killed. Sex was their primary reason for going to the room and sex didn't happen. Maybe sleep did instead."

"Something did," Walt said.

I filled Jane in on the latest developments.

She nibbled dry toast as I talked.

"Oz is okay?" she said when I finished.

"Yes," I said. "A little worse for wear, but okay."

"This kid on the bike is long gone by now," Jane said. "Or he switched out the bike for a car."

"Probably."

"He's proof that Simms stumbled into something other than a good time in Room 15," Jane said.

"Speaking of, are we ready?" I said.

A few minutes later, Jane, Walt and I sat on the tiny sofa in Room 15 and stared at the bed in front of us.

"And?" Walt said.

"Jane, let me see that list of evidence Forensics removed from the room," I said.

Jane had a stack of folders on her lap. She passed me the one I asked for. I read the list of removed items and saw what I missed the first time.

"One small metal screw," I said.

"What?" Walt said. "Where?"

"Removed as evidence," I said. "One small metal screw."

Jane looked at the list in my hands.

"Could have been here before he checked in," she said. "Could be from the previous occupant. Could be from anything."

"Could be," I said.

We stared at the bed, the wall, the furniture.

"What has tiny metal screws in it?" I said.

"Almost everything," Walt said. "Including my wife's left ankle. It's a real treat at airports when it sets off the alarms."

I looked above the bed. I saw what was bothering me, what was nagging at me in the back of my mind. Sometimes you look so close you don't see what you're looking at.

I stood up. I stepped up onto the bed and inspected the two air vents. The left vent was held in place by four tiny screws. The right vent had three. One screw was missing.

Walt and Jane came on the bed and looked at the right vent.

"Son of a bitch," Walt said.

Walt had a pocket tool and used the mini screwdriver to remove the three screws from the right vent, then pulled it away from the wall. The thin layer of dust on the floor of the vent had a two-inch square traced in it.

"Somebody put something in here," Jane said.

"That somebody was cold while they were waiting and turned up the heat," I said. "They came in and that somebody probably hid in the shower. Did Forensics dust inside the shower stall for footprints and fingerprints?"

Jane and Walt stared at me.

"No," Jane finally said. "But they will."

I stepped off the bed and looked at the angle of the slat holes in the left vent. They were aimed downward toward the bed.

"A mini camera," I said. "To record the event."

"Are you saying that Jon Hughes installed a camera to record his own murder?" Jane said. "Or his sexcapades?"

"No," Walt said. "But whoever murdered Jon Hughes did."

Jane and Walt stepped off the bed.

We looked up at the air vent.

"Why didn't he kill Simms?" Jane said. "Why leave a witness?"

"He was interrupted before he got the chance," Walt said. "By the police knocking on the door."

"The couple in the next room called 911," Jane said.

"After they heard the thump," Walt said.

"And he goes out the bathroom window," I said. "Closing it from the outside."

"What was the thump?" Jane said.

"Anybody in the next room?" I said.

"I'll find out," Jane said.

Ten minutes later, Jane was on her cell phone in the adjacent room.

"What am I listening for?" she said.

"Put down the phone, get in bed and tell me if you hear this," I said.

I put my cell phone on the bed and looked at Walt.

"Hear what?" he said.

I grabbed Walt by his suit jacket and shoved him backward as hard as I could into the wall, resulting in a loud thud.

"What the fuck are you . . . ?" Walt said.

He looked at me as I dropped my hands. His eyes told me that he got it, then he slowly turned and looked at the wall.

I picked up my phone.

"Jane?"

"If I was in a coma," Jane said. "That would have woken me up."

"They fought," Walt said as Jane returned.

"Over what?" she said.

Our eyes went to the bed.

"Simms," I said. "She was the prize."

CHAPTER 53

"Doesn't make any fucking sense," Walt said as he drove me back to Janet's.

"Maybe not now," I said. "Maybe not to us. Think about it. Five men murdered and all of them are from Sacred Heart from the same time period and they all knew each other."

"Say you're right," Walt said. "Say a kid from the home has a hard-on for this group, how do the older women fit into it? Besides that, there's no evidence the Stousser kid was with an older woman or anybody else when he was killed. Stousser breaks the pattern."

"Maybe, but the circumstantial evidence is too much to ignore," I said. "And we don't know for sure if Stousser was alone before he was killed."

"Jesus Christ, the sick sonofabitch is filming his murders," Walt said.

I looked at Walt.

"Or making snuff films," I said. "That's a possibility."

"Oh, fuck," Walt said.

"Do me a favor," I said. "See where there's a demand for snuff films. We might get lucky and find us a murderer."

We arrived at Janet's home and Walt pulled into the driveway.

"What are you going to do?" he said.

"First, I'm going to give my daughter and Janet a big kiss," I said. "Then I'm going to see Clark. After that, I'm going to see Simms. Then I'm coming back here."

"I'll call you later," Walt said.

Regan and Mark were tossing a Frisbee in the backyard. Janet and Sister Mary Martin were having coffee at the patio table under the watchful eye of one of Walt's detectives.

I greeted Janet with a kiss as I took a seat at the patio table.

"She looks happy," I said as I watched Regan catch a long toss from Mark.

"Yes, she does," Janet said. "Have time for lunch?"

"I'm only staying a minute."

"A home cooked dinner later tonight?"

"Absolutely."

"Good," Janet said. "Be back in time to help me home-cook it."

"Yes, mother," I said and left Janet with another kiss.

I called Clark on my cell phone and he told me to meet him in superior court.

"I had to file papers on another matter," Clark said when I met him in the courthouse waiting room.

"You have time for some coffee?" I said. "This could take a while."

I filled two containers with coffee in the courthouse cafeteria and we found a small table against the wall.

Clark listened while I brought him up to speed. I ended with, "Jane is having the vent and cover dusted for prints, same for the shower. Walt is doing an Interpol check for snuff films on the black market."

"Good God," Clark said. He shook his head. "Snuff films."

"As a dishonest lawyer who can be bought by the mob, who do you have at AP that can write a story for us?" I said.

Clark stared at me for a moment.

"You never fail to amaze me, Detective," he said. "A story about five men from the same home murdered in similar fashion is sure to garner a great deal of attention."

"And shift some of it away from Simms," I said.

"And paint a big, black bulls-eye on your back," Clark said.

"If we're lucky," I said.

"You're sure?"

"I'm sure."

My cell phone rang. It was Jane with an update.

"Forensics got a clean set of prints off the grill interior," she said. "They don't belong to Jon Hughes, but no match for them found in the system yet."

"Doesn't matter," I said. "The plot thickens. We now can say there's a definite possibility a third party was in the room with Simms and Hughes."

I hung up and looked at Clark.

"Right?" I said.

Clark nodded.

"Just make sure you watch your back," he said. "I'm starting to sort of like you."

"Call you later," I said. "I'm going to give Simms a heads-up on the story."

I stood up from the table.

"Hey, Bekker?" Clark said. "I know we've had our differences in the past, but I wouldn't like it if you wound up dead."

"I wouldn't either," I said. "So I'll do my best to stay alive."

CHAPTER 54

Simms was doing laps in the Olympic-sized pool when I arrived.

Ever the sun-worshipping bunny, Campbell was topless on a recliner.

She raised the back of the recliner when I took the one to her left.

"I need to talk to Simms," I said.

Campbell reached for her cigarettes on the table between the chairs and lit one.

"She's doing laps," Campbell said as she blew smoke from her nostrils.

"I see that. Can she stop doing laps?"

"When she reaches twenty-five."

"What's she up to now?"

"Eleven. I've been keeping count."

"Can't she stop long enough for me to talk to her?"

"She could, but she won't," Campbell said. "The woman is possessed with her workouts."

"How long will another fourteen laps take?"

"About as long as it takes for us to have a drink and then go into the cabana over there for a quick fuck," Campbell said. "Interested?"

"No to both."

"Then I guess you'll just have to read a magazine," Campbell said, and reclined her chair and picked up a copy of *Vogue*.

I removed the charger from my pocket, stuck a tube in my mouth and another in the charging slot.

Twenty minutes and two vapor tubes later, a naked Simms emerged from the pool. She climbed up the ladder and stood for a moment, shook her hair and looked at me without a hint of embarrassment. Her body from head to toe was lean, hard muscle. Then she grabbed a white robe off a chair, slipped it on and walked to the chair on my left.

"We need to talk," I said.

"Alone?" Simms said.

"That's up to her," I said. "What I have to tell you will make the news this time tomorrow."

"Intriguing," Campbell said as she sat up. "Do go on."

I gave them the short version.

"I don't remember a third person in the room," Simms said. "Of course, I was passed out for quite a while, so it's possible."

"Was she set up and if so, for what?" Campbell said.

"I don't know," I said. "What I do know is someone is targeting former residents of Sacred Heart and that four of the five have involved attractive older women."

"Did they sweep the fifth victim's apartment for traces of a woman?" Simms said.

"Traces?" Campbell said.

"Faint perfume in the air, speckles of makeup on the sink, things like that," Simms said.

"No, but they weren't aware of any of this when the body was discovered," I said. "I'll ask Walt to make a few calls later. My guess is they'll find something to make it five for five."

"I hate to fearmonger here, but is this something we should be worried about?" Campbell said. "What you said about the man who attacked your friend, what's to stop him from coming here?"

"He doesn't know where you are, for one thing," I said. "And you have a half dozen armed men around the clock for another."

"How do you know you weren't followed?" Campbell said.

"If you're that afraid, I'll make other arrangements for a safe-house," I said.

"I didn't say I was afraid," Campbell said. "But I am concerned for me as well as Carly. That said, I have a suggestion if you'll listen."

"I'm listening," I said.

"I usually vacation at the Villa in Palm Beach this time of year," Campbell said. "Carly can go with me as my guest until this mess is sorted out. My men go with me and the place is a fortress."

"I can't ask you to put yourself in that kind of position," Simms said.

"You already have," Campbell said. "Besides, I have to do something to earn my half mil and Palm Beach is beautiful this time of year."

Simms looked at me.

"What do you think?" she said.

"You've surrendered your passport and driver's license?" I said.

"Locked away in Clark's safe," Simms said.

"I'll talk to Clark," I said. "If he agrees, I think it might be a good idea."

"We'll charter a plane and take the bodyguards," Campbell said. "And I'll feel better and safer about the whole thing and so will you."

"I'll call you later," I said.

Campbell stood up.

"Now that we've settled that, I'm going to do some laps," she said. "Care to join me, Mr. Bekker?"

"I never learned how to swim," I said.

"One is never too old to learn new things," Campbell said and dove into the pool.

CHAPTER 55

"Clark's okay with Simms moving to Palm Beach?" Walt said.

"He ran it by the judge," I said. "No objections provided she checks in weekly until the trial and stays put in the complex."

"And you?" Walt said.

"What about me?"

We were at the patio table in Janet's backyard. Not quite ten p.m., we sat in darkness and sipped coffee.

The floodlight suddenly came on.

Oz hobbled out to the table.

"What about him?" Oz said.

"He's a first-class brick head, that's what about him," Walt said.

"You won't get an argument from me," Oz said.

"What are you doing out of bed?" I said.

"I'm getting bed sores," Oz said. "Besides, I'm feeling well enough to go home."

Walt and I exchanged glances.

"What?" Oz said.

"The brick head is setting himself up as a human target," Walt said. "Which means it isn't safe for you to go home just yet."

Oz looked at me. "Target?"

"For a little while," I said.

"Until what?" Oz said. "I can go home or you get yourself killed?"

Mark stuck his head out of the open kitchen door.

"Uncle Jack, Regan cheats at video baseball," Mark said. "There's no way I could lose three out of four to a girl."

"What time did your mother say you needed to be in bed?" I said.

"Umm, midnight," Mark lied with a straight face.

"Boy, I'm gonna whip your ass," Oz said.

"Maybe it was ten-thirty," Mark said.

"More like ten," Oz said.

"Can't blame a guy for trying," Mark said.

Oz stood up. "Yeah, I can."

"I'm going, I'm going," Mark said and disappeared.

"I'm just going to the bathroom," Oz said and entered the kitchen through the sliding doors.

Walt looked at me. "You sure you know what you're doing?"

"No, do you?"

"Joke if you want to, Jack," Walt said. "Just remember one thing. I'm the slob who has to tell your daughter and Janet that you're dead."

I looked at Walt.

"Aw, fuck," Walt said. "I got your back."

"I already know that, Walt," I said.

"Just watch your front is all I'm saying."

"Consider it watched."

"I'm going home," Walt said. "Maybe my wife might recognize me."

I sat alone for a little while and smoked a vapor tube. When I entered the kitchen, I closed the sliding doors and heard Sister Mary Martin say from the living room, "You would cheat against a nun?"

I poked my head in the living room. Regan was beating the nun in video baseball.

Regan turned and looked at me.

She winked.

"I'm a nun," Sister Mary Martin said in frustration. "Two things you can't do in baseball. Cry and cheat a nun."

I grinned and winked at Regan.

I sat at the kitchen table with a fresh mug of coffee.

If only the rules of life were as simple as the rules of baseball.

It was time to break the rules.

All of them.

And cheating was allowed.

CHAPTER 56

Abner's gunsmith shop was the choice of law enforcement within a fifty-mile radius of its location for nearly thirty years. Even out of state and feds frequented Abner's for their crime-fighting needs.

This was true because Abner was a master craftsman when it came to handgun and long-gun weaponry. It was said he could make a pistol from all plastic parts and a full-size cannon using plastic tubes and hairspray. I don't know who said it or if it was true, but a better gunsmith would be hard to find.

An electronic police siren sounded for a few seconds when I opened the door and walked into the shop. Racks of long guns and shotguns stood secured by chains and cables behind a long glass counter. The counter held dozens of pistols and revolvers. Behind the counter, a bottom shelf was lined with boxes of ammunition.

Abner came out from the back room and stood behind the waist-high counter. A thin man of about sixty, Abner had not a strand of hair on his head and a thick walrus mustache that covered his upper lip.

From behind clear safety goggles, he studied me for a moment.

"You look familiar," he said. "We done business before?"

"About fifteen years ago, I was a sergeant with Special Crimes," I said. "I bought a Beretta 9 and holster from you. You adjusted the trigger pull and built a custom-made silencer."

"Was a sergeant with Special Crimes," Abner said. "What are you now?"

I removed my driver's license, state pistol permit and private investigator's license from my wallet and set them on the counter.

Abner inspected them carefully for signs of fraud.

"I remember you now," he said. "What can I help you with?"

"The .45 I carry now is slow," I said. "I'd like something lighter, faster and with a silencer."

"I can't sell you a silencer," Abner said. "Only authorized law enforcement can carry and use a silencer in this state unless you have a special permit. Do you have one?"

"No."

"Take you six months to get it."

"I don't have six months."

"Then what else can I do for you?"

"Let me see a Glock 9MM," I said. "With fifteen-round magazines."

Abner used a key to unlock a glass door. He slid it open, removed a Glock 17, and set it on the counter.

"Holds seventeen rounds, is lightweight and solid as the day is long," Abner said. "Even fires underwater."

"I'll take it and four extra magazines," I said. "And two boxes of ammunition."

Abner stared at me for a moment.

"You expecting trouble?" he said.

"Are you familiar with the Simms murder case?" I said.

"Who isn't?"

"I'm the investigator for the law firm defending her," I said. "My entire family is under death threats as well as Simms."

"That's why the silencer?" Abner said.

"If it comes down to it and I have to defend my family and Simms, I'd rather have an edge," I said.

"I can't sell you one," Abner said. "Since you're no longer on the job. How are you with machinery?"

"Good."

"I can sell you the parts," Abner said. "What you do with them is your business."

"What do I owe you?" I said.

CHAPTER 57

It didn't take much to assemble the silencer and machine it to fit the Glock 17. A few hours' work with some tools and I was ready to test-fire it. I picked up an archery target and set it fifty feet behind the trailer. A foot thick of compressed Styrofoam wouldn't stop a .44 Magnum or .357 at that distance, but a 9MM round slowed by a silencer shouldn't be a problem.

I didn't aim.

No need at fifty feet.

I raised the Glock and fired seventeen rounds at the target.

The noise level was little more than a soft cough.

I lowered the Glock and walked to the target. There was a nice group around six inches in diameter. Not one of the seventeen rounds exited the back. Penetration was about ten inches thick, more than enough to do the job on human flesh.

I returned to the trailer, brewed a pot of coffee and carried it and a gun-cleaning kit out to the lounge chair.

I removed the silencer and field-stripped the Glock.

I smoked a vapor tube, sipped coffee and cleaned the parts.

Someone would come for me.

Soon.

The story written by Clark's AP contact took care of that. He went into detail to highlight the similarities of the five Sacred Heart victims, planting the seed that Simms might be innocent after all. I was named as the investigator hired by Clark who made the connection.

Who would come for me?

The kid on the bike?

Whoever hired the kid to tail me?

Somebody.

More than one?

Somebody.

I felt better about being a human target with Walt covering my back, but only a little. Walt was background material. Step too far into the light and it blows your cover.

Maybe a lot of somebodies would come?

Maybe if they got to me, they would get to my family?

Maybe I couldn't allow that to happen.

Somebody somewhere had it in for former residents of Sacred Heart and I might have foiled their future plans.

It came down to a classic case of kill the messenger.

I was the messenger.

I wiped the parts of the Glock and reassembled them. I carefully loaded the five magazines with 9MM ammunition, inserted one magazine, racked the slide and pushed the safety to the on position.

I cleaned the silencer and slipped it into my pocket.

It was time to go about my business.

And wait for somebody to try to kill me.

And hope that I was good enough not to let that happen.

CHAPTER 58

The night air coming off the ocean had a slight chill to it, but not enough to warrant the bonfire I had going in the garbage can in front of the trailer.

As they say in the movies, it was strictly for effect.

The fire could be seen for at least a mile in all directions, announcing to anyone watching that I was indeed home.

I ate some dinner in the lounge chair and listened to the waves crash and break down at the very dark beach. The moon had yet to rise and a billion stars were visible overhead.

I kept my eyes off the fire to keep my night vision intact.

I drank coffee to keep my brain alert.

I avoided looking at my watch to keep time from slowing down.

That's the trick to passing time quickly.

You pay no attention to it and it pays no attention to you.

A lot of years ago when I was in my second year on the job, I was pulled off uniform duty to assist detectives with a stakeout. I was green and made stupid rookie mistakes. The stakeout took place inside a white, unmarked van. I drank cup after cup of coffee and didn't bring a coffee can to relieve myself in. I kept looking at my watch and the more I looked at it, the slower time passed. The more time slowed, the greater I needed to pee. It was an uncomfortable watch to say the least.

My cell phone on the card table rang.

It was Janet.

"I'm off at midnight," she said. "I'm coming over."

"No," I said. "It isn't safe right now around here. Go straight home."

"Damn you, Jack," Janet said. "Do I have to beg for a little attention?"

"I miss you and I miss Regan and Mark, but I can't do what I need to do if I have to worry about your safety first," I said.

"But . . ."

"No buts," I said. "That's it. The topic is closed."

Janet sighed. "I know you're right, of course," she said. "It's just difficult for me to understand why you're the one who has to risk his life for the sake of a stranger. At least the police are paid to take risks. You seem to do it for fun, and that worries me. A lot."

It was my turn to sigh.

"There's nothing fun about waiting in the dark for a stranger to come along and try to kill you," I said.

Janet gasped softly.

"I probably shouldn't have said that," I said. "I'm sorry."

"Asshole," Janet said and hung up.

I set the cell phone on the card table, removed a tube from the charger and picked up the phone again when Janet called back.

"That's not what I meant to say," Janet said. "What I meant to say is I love you."

"And I love you," I said.

"That doesn't mean you aren't an asshole, though, because you are."

"And I still love you."

"You will be careful?"

"As much as is humanly possible."

"Call me in the morning to let me know you're still alive."

"I will."

"Good night."

"Kiss Regan for me."

"I will."

I set the phone on the card table, got up and added a few logs to the bonfire.

I sat and smoked another tube. I knew Walt was out there somewhere, covering my back. Was that enough? A sniper with a night-vision scope could pick me off from a distance of a quarter mile, the bonfire was so bright.

So far, guns were not an issue.

Bare hands and a letter opener were the weapons used.

That told me the killer wanted to get close and see what was going on when he snuffed out a life. It told me there was a certain amount of pleasure involved. Pleasure derived from revenge, perhaps. Revenge for wrongs done to a child now grown up and looking for some payback.

I wasn't part of that, so maybe killing me brought no sweet revenge. I was just in the way. Why not take me out quick with one well-placed shot?

Waiting is a game of nerves.

Most aren't cut out for it. Most will bend as time passes and eventually break. It's not a question of if, but of when.

I sat and drank coffee as the bonfire in the trashcan burned itself out and then I sat in darkness for a while. I used the time to think, to sort things out in my mind.

What would happen to Regan if I were suddenly gone?

Would she continue to grow into an adult, or regress back to a five-year-old mentality?

Janet would be there for her, I knew that. Who would be there for Janet?

I lost my wife because I wasn't there for her. I nearly lost my daughter for the same reason. Why would I put myself in a posi-tion to allow that to happen again?

I peered into the pitch black in front of me and listened to the soft waves smack against the beach. The tide was out now, its power minimized.

I decided to call it a night.

I entered the trailer, locked the door and drew the curtains.

I opened the trap door under the kitchen table and dropped down to the sand below. I closed the trap door, rolled out behind the trailer, and stood in darkness for a moment.

I walked the hundred yards to Oz's trailer, rolled under it, and opened the trap door. I pulled myself up into the kitchen, shut the trap door and twisted the bolt lock closed.

Satisfied nothing would go down tonight, I flopped onto the sofa and closed my eyes. Within moments, I felt myself drift off into a dark and dreamless sleep.

CHAPTER 59

For three days and nights, I went about my business as normally as possible given the circumstances.

I wore a bulletproof vest under my shirt and concealed it with a suit jacket. It was uncomfortable and hot, but knowing it would stop a small-arms slug at even close range gave me a false sense of security.

False because there was nothing to stop a head shot, nothing to prevent my legs being shot out from under me, nothing to keep me alive if he wanted me dead. Every cop, every soldier knows that feeling to be true.

I walked to town, had lunch at a diner, picked up a newspaper and read it on a bench in a shady little park nearby. I window-shopped, lingered at the food market, lingered even longer over coffee at an outdoor café.

Nobody paid me the slightest bit of attention.

I was just a guy with time on his hands.

I didn't call Walt.

I knew he was out there.

I didn't call Janet.

I knew she was at home or work, and worrying about me. No sense heightening her worry with an *I'm fine* phone call.

A call would only maximize her worry.

We both knew that no news was good news.

I walked back to my trailer at a leisurely pace. I removed my shoes and stayed close to the beach. The sand was hot from the sun, but not to the point it was uncomfortable. I reached my rusty lawn chair, took a seat, and replaced my shoes.

My back was covered with sweat and it stuck to the hot plastic backing of the lawn chair. I could feel the weight of the vest against my back, heavy and growing heavier.

I squinted into the sun and looked for something out of place. Surfers rode soft waves. Gulls rummaged for scraps. A few men in waders fished for stripers. Not an eye cast my way.

There was no point looking for Walt. He could be fifty feet behind me and I wouldn't spot him, he was that good.

I stood up and used my key to unlock the door to my trailer. I took a step into the tiny living room and had a split second to react before an explosion rocked my head and my face hit the floor and it all went black.

CHAPTER 60

I wasn't dead.

Just gagged with a hood over my head, tied with rope to a hardback wooden chair.

A thousand thoughts flashed through my mind, none of them good. In the situation I found myself in, it's difficult to have a good thought.

They outsmarted Walt and he's the best, better than I am. They were either very good or very lucky.

Maybe both.

Questions raced through my mind.

How far were they willing to go and for what gain?

Would they let me live or kill me as an afterthought to whatever game they were playing?

Any experienced cop will tell you, crimes are committed for profit. The risk is outweighed by the gain. The higher the gain, the greater the risk, but the risk is never outweighed by what is stood to gain. Without gain, crime doesn't exist. What gain was there in kidnapping me?

What gain was there in killing me?

What gain was there in letting me live?

My hands and feet were tied to the chair but the chair wasn't secured to the floor. I rocked it side to side until I had enough momentum to topple the chair and fall to my left onto the floor.

It was bare.

I landed with a loud crash.

It hurt, but I was ready for the impact.

I wrestled with the ropes around my wrists.

I didn't get very far before someone was in the room with me. That someone kicked me in the ribs. Several times. If you've never been kicked in the ribs, besides the intense pain, it instantly takes the air from your lungs.

"Where you going, asshole?" a male voice said.

Hands gripped the chair and righted me. They yanked the hood from my head and tore the duct tape from my lips.

I screamed as the tape ripped away skin.

He quieted my scream with a kick to my jaw.

The chair fell backward and my head smacked against the floor.

"Now hush," the man said. "You stupid fuck."

I sucked in air and tasted blood in my mouth. The salt stung the sensitive skin where the tape had removed a layer of flesh. I stole a quick look around the room. There wasn't a stick of furniture in it except for the chair I was bound to. The walls and roof were metal. There were no windows. A light fixture on the ceiling provided yellowish illumination.

The man grabbed the chair and righted it again. He looked at me. I looked at him. He was young, around twenty-four or so, tall and muscular in a tank top.

"Let me guess," I said. "You grew up in Sacred Heart with all the other unwanted mutts?"

He grinned and shook his head at me.

"You think you're so fucking smart," he said. "You leave a trail of breadcrumbs Stevie Wonder could follow."

"My friend knows I'm missing by now," I said.

"The cop?" he said. "Had a little car accident. Nothing serious. Just enough to avert his attention."

"He'll find you," I said. "He won't quit until he finds you."

"You're missing the point here," he said. "I'm asking the questions."

"Won't do you a bit of good," I said.

"No?" he said. "Maybe if we check out that juicy nurse you hang around with, or toss a ball around with her kid. That retard daughter of yours is looking pretty juicy herself these days, huh, Dad? Seems ripe for the taking, if you follow me."

I closed my eyes.

"Where is she?" he said. "The lady prosecutor."

I opened my eyes.

"Fuck you," I said.

He sighed at me.

"Right about now you're probably wondering how we got the drop on you," he said. "Being such an experienced cop and all. Thing is, you gave everybody and their mother your business card and phone number. It's amazing what you can find out by computer these days."

"I wasn't exactly hiding," I said. "But now that we've found each other, what do you want from me?"

"Her," he said. "Weren't you fucking listening? We want her, the bitch prosecutor."

"Simms?"

"It's impossible for anyone to be this fucking stupid," he said. "Yes, Simms, fucking Simms."

"What for?"

"That's our business."

"Not if you want me to hand her over to you, it isn't."

"You'll hand her over."

"Or what?"

"We'll kill that juicy nurse you're so fond of," he said. "Or maybe that sissy kid of hers will have a fatal accident. Or . . . we'll take that pretty little daughter of yours and rape and sodomize her until her eyes bleed and make you watch while we do it. That's 'or what.' "

I stared at him.

"It won't work on me, orphan," I said. "Say whatever you want, I won't lose my cool."

He looked at me. He blinked a few times and I knew at that moment I had him.

"You what . . . what did you call me?"

"Orphan," I said. "That's what you are, aren't you?"

"Fuck you, old man," he snarled. "Give us that stinking bitch or we'll start with your daughter and work our way up from there."

"Angry at the world because Mommy got herself knocked up at fifteen and dumped your unwanted ass in Sacred Heart," I said. "That's you, kid, an unwanted bastard."

"Shut up," he snapped. "Shut the fuck up."

"No tit milk as a baby," I said. "Now you probably can't get it up for a woman without slapping her around and you're mad at the whole world because Mommy dumped your useless ass. Or maybe you're gay from living and taking showers with all those guys?"

His eyes were suddenly ablaze.

"I'll fucking kill you!" he shouted.

"And her location dies with me," I said. "Orphan."

"Don't call me that," he snarled.

"I don't have a tit, but I do have nipples," I said. "You can suckle them if you'd like."

"Fuck you," he screamed and punched me in the face.

The chair rocked, but held.

Blood ran down my nose in twin red streams into my mouth.

I spit red.

"Is Simms your mommy?" I said. "That's what you do, track down your mommies and murder them for their sins? You're a

fucking loser, kid, a gutless, limp-dick, sissy-boy orphan bastard."

He slapped me twice across the face.

"That slut is not my mother!" he screamed. "She's not, do
you hear me?"

"Then what do you want her for?" I said. "Orphan."

He screamed and went into a spin kick. The heel of his right
foot hit me like a club on the left side of my jaw. The impact
knocked the chair over. I hit the floor hard and bounced.

But not hard enough to break the chair.

I ate the pain and forced a grin as I looked up at him.

"Is that what you do, track down mommies who abandoned
their babies and kill them?" I said. "Is Simms your mommy?
I've seen her naked, you know. She could feed you for weeks
with what she's got. That's what you want, isn't it? Mommy's
love."

"You motherfucker!" he screamed. "Shut the fuck up."

He kicked me several more times. In the face, ribs, stomach.

I forced myself not to pass out.

He quit kicking me and stepped back, breathing hard from
his exertion.

"Now where the fuck is she?" he said as he righted the chair
and glared at me. "Last time I'm gonna ask, then I'll pay your
daughter a little visit and bring pliers and a blowtorch with me.
I'll go fucking medieval on her. She'll beg me to kill her when
I'm through."

"You know, maybe if you had a mommy and were raised
right, you might not be so fucking stupid," I said. "You worthless loser."

"I guess you don't give a shit about your kid," he said.

"Who came up with this little orphan boys club, anyway?" I
said. "The kid on the bike? It sure wasn't you. A brainless moron
like you couldn't find his own dick if it came with instructions

and a map."

"I told him this was a bad idea, grabbing you," he said. "He wouldn't fucking listen, that fucking idiot."

"Who wouldn't listen?" I said.

He looked at me and a thin smile crossed his lips.

"I'm not telling you shit, you dimwit," I said. "And do you know why?"

"Why?"

"Because you didn't bother to hide your face," I said. "That means no matter what, you're going to kill me, so kill away, if you got the balls. Momma's boy."

"Oh, I got the balls, asshole," he said. "You wouldn't be the first."

"No, who was the first?" I said. "Hughes? Lind? Who, you worthless, gutless bastard orphan."

He glared hate at me.

"She's your mommy, isn't she?" I said.

"No."

"A hot middle-aged mommy who you hate so much, you want to fuck her to get even," I said.

"Shut up!" he screamed. "Shut the fuck up!"

"Isn't that right," I said. "Orphan."

He lost all control then and kicked me in the chest. The chair hit the floor and the impact knocked the wind out of me.

"She's not my mother!" he yelled and kicked me a half dozen times.

I closed my eyes and went limp.

"Fucking moron asshole," he spat. "Look at you now, asshole."

I stayed motionless.

I could hear his out-of-control breathing start to slow. His footsteps echoed on the floor. Then the door opened and slammed shut.

I had to move fast. I didn't know how long it would take him to cool off and return. The beating the wooden chair took had loosened its structure. It didn't take much for me to crack it open at the back. I bounced and it split down the middle, freeing my hands.

A few more bounces and the entire chair fell apart. The knots in the rope loosened and I slipped out and freed my legs.

I jumped to my feet and grabbed a chair leg.

Without a window, I couldn't see outside. I didn't know if it was night or day, country or city.

I hugged the wall beside the door with the chair leg at the ready. I didn't have my watch, but at least two minutes passed by my count before the door opened.

I didn't mean to kill him.

He was no good to me dead.

I aimed the chair leg at his nose. A broken nose causes a great deal of pain, causes instant disorientation and makes it easy to disable a person, but does no real damage.

He caught sight of the chair leg an instant before it struck, turned and took the full impact on the soft flesh of the throat.

He was dead before he hit the floor.

I knew it from the sound the chair leg made when it struck.

I knew it from the impact a dead body makes when it falls.

There's no life to it.

There was no life to his.

I looked outside. It was night and pitch dark.

I knelt down and took his pulse. There was none. I went through his pockets and came up empty. No wallet, ID, money. Nothing.

I rolled him over. Clutched tightly in his right fist was a tiny cell phone. I pried it loose and checked for a signal. I stepped outside and dialed Walt's cell phone number.

He answered on the first ring.

"Lieutenant Grimes," Walt said.

"It's Jack," I said.

"Where are you?" Walt said. "I've been looking for you for . . ."

"Shut up and listen," I said. "I need you to come get me right away and bring Forensics."

"Where?"

I looked up at the sign over the long row of storage compartments.

"Hunt's Point Rental Storage Facility," I said. "Compartment 24."

"What the fuck are you doing out there?"

"Just get here quick," I said.

"That's an hour from . . ."

"I'll wait," I said. "I have nowhere else to go. And bring coffee. Lots and lots of coffee."

"Anything else?" Walt said. "Maybe a nice lemon Danish?"

"Cigarettes," I said. "Bring some real goddamn cigarettes."

"On my way," Walt said.

CHAPTER 61

I sat with Walt in his wife's car and sucked down a cruller as I gave him as many details as I could remember. I sipped coffee to wash down the donut. The hot liquid burned my swollen lips and bleeding gums.

"They cut me off on the way to your place," Walt said. "An old pickup took out the passenger door. While you were having lunch, I needed to make a pit stop. I should have brought a coffee can. I'm sorry, Jack. I blew it."

"No, it gave them the opportunity to make their move," I said. "I blew it by killing this punk."

"Is he bike boy?"

"Probably."

Walt sipped coffee and looked out his window for a moment.

"Is Simms his mother?" he said.

"DNA testing will tell us that," I said.

Walt shook his head.

"So a group of teenage boys starts to come of age and they're seething with rage over the fact Mommy doesn't love them, and they do what?" Walt said. "Form a kill mom of the week club?"

"Seems that way," I said as I polished off the cruller.

"Why kill the boys?" Walt said. "If they're setting up Mommy as targets, why kill the boys?"

I shook my head as I opened the pack of cigarettes Walt picked up for me.

"And Simms wasn't killed by the third person in Room 15,

Hughes was," Walt said. "Why let her live if she was the target? Even if he panicked and ran out the bathroom window when the police arrived, he might have had time to finish her off first."

"You can't humiliate someone if they're passed out drunk," I said. "He might have wanted her awake. Bring matches?"

Walt fished matches out of a pocket.

"He was waiting for Simms to wake up before he killed her," Walt said. "So she would know. You're right. What's the fun of humiliating someone if they don't know they're being disgraced?"

I struck the match and lit the cigarette.

"He waited and waited, but Simms was just too drunk and then the police arrived," Walt said. "And by then it was too late and he beat it out the bathroom window."

I inhaled smoke.

There was nothing like the real thing.

"He figured there would be a next time," Walt said. "Given her track record and reputation."

I blew a smoke ring and watched it fade into the roof of the car.

"So who's behind all this?" Walt said.

"It's not that kid in there," I said. "Emotionally, he's barely above sixteen. No car, how did I get here?"

"Someone is waiting for a call they won't get," Walt said. "By now they realize that call isn't coming. By now they're in the wind."

"He said it's amazing what you can do with computers, or something like that," I said. "Somebody with a great deal of knowledge with computers is behind this. Somebody who can access records, pirate their way into classified documents and find out who is the mother of whom. Somebody who can find out everything about me and set me up like this and take you out in the process."

"The Hughes kid was an expert," Walt said.

"Yeah, but he's dead."

"Along with four others."

I took a sip of coffee, then inhaled through my very sore nose. "Who were probably part of this merry little band of brothers."

"Why kill them if they were members of the club?"

We looked at each other for a moment.

"They got cold feet," Walt said.

"About what?" I said.

Walt shook his head.

"Maybe they couldn't go through with killing their victims?" I said. "Maybe the brain behind all this decided to punish them for their failure by killing them along with the women."

"Except the Stousser kid was killed in his dorm room," Walt said. "Alone, and that breaks the pattern."

"What if the Stousser kid decided to quit the little club after the story went national?" I said. "He would have to be removed to keep the club a secret."

"He would," Walt agreed.

"What would you bet Hughes's laptop contains enough vital information to break this egg wide open," I said.

"I wouldn't take that bet," Walt said.

The door to the compartment opened and the team of forensic investigators stepped out. One of them approached the car.

"Lieutenant, we're finished here," he said. "We have prints, hair and everything else we can document."

"Did you get a DNA sample?" I said.

He shook his head.

"Get one," I said.

He looked at Walt.

Walt nodded.

The team reentered the compartment and closed the door.

I looked at Walt.

"They took DNA from Hughes?" I said.

"Jane's people did."

"Can we get a sample from Simms without her knowing?" I said.

Walt looked at me. His face was blank for a moment, then it sunk in and he sighed.

"Aw, Christ," Walt said. "Hughes was sent to kill his mother."

I shook my head.

"Hughes was sent to seduce and have sex with his mother," I said. "And to record the event on camera as a final humiliation, and then kill her."

Walt closed his eyes for a moment. When he opened them, he looked at me.

"It's a sad world we live in, Jack," he said. "And sometimes I hate my fucking job."

I removed a second cigarette from the pack and lit it with a paper match.

The forensics team returned.

"Got it, Lieutenant," one of them said. "Want me to call the ME and have the body removed?"

"I'll do that," Walt said. "You guys get to the lab and start processing. Nobody goes home until it's done."

We sat in the car, drank coffee and waited for the ambulance to arrive.

"Whoever left this kid to babysit me is behind all this," I said. "If I coughed up Simms, they would have left me for dead. Maybe that kid wouldn't have done it, but somebody would have."

By the time the ambulance and ME arrived, it was close to dawn. After they carted the kid's body away, Walt and I sat for a few minutes and watched the sunrise.

It's funny how the light of a new day can wash away the stink of even the darkest night.

"Where do we go from here?" Walt said. "We have a dead kid, no evidence of anything that remotely proves our theory and someone who wants to kill Simms and you to boot still running around loose."

"I need some sleep, Walt," I said.

"You and me both."

"Want to have breakfast first?"

"Let's get takeout," Walt said. "You ain't exactly pretty at the moment."

CHAPTER 62

Walt and I were stuffing our faces with egg and sausage biscuit sandwiches when I spotted a dark sedan entering the beach.

I looked at Walt.

"When did you call Janet?" I said.

"When I went inside to order breakfast," Walt said. "Looking at your face, I figured you could use a little medical attention and I knew you wouldn't go to a hospital and I doubt you have a private doctor."

I polished off the sandwich and washed it down with coffee.

"I didn't need a hospital before, but I will after she gets here," I said.

"Want me to leave?"

"And who will protect me?"

With one of Walt's detectives behind the wheel and another riding shotgun, the sedan arrived and parked beside my Marquis.

Before the engine shut off, Janet was out and walking toward me.

"How could you . . . ?" she said and gasped when she saw me.

"It's not as bad as it looks," Walt said.

"You shut up, you fucking imbecile," Janet snapped. "You call this protecting him? The nun would do a better job of protecting him."

"Yes, ma'am," Walt said meekly.

I stood up from my lawn chair.

Janet slapped me across the face. "Idiot," she said.

She balled her hands into fists and punched me in the chest.

"Look at you, just look at you!" she shouted as she continued punching me.

Janet is a powerful woman and her punches hurt, especially the ones that landed on my nose and mouth.

"That isn't helping any," Walt said. "Unless you think you can fix a broken nose by punching it back into position."

Janet lowered her fists and looked at me.

"Coffee's fresh," I said. "Want a cup?"

She threw her hands in the air and sat down in Oz's chair. She glared at Walt as I went into the trailer for another mug.

I returned in a few seconds with a mug full of coffee and set it on the card table next to Janet.

She looked at me.

"You child," she said. "Go on and get yourself killed."

"I didn't get killed," I said. "I'm not even seriously hurt, except for the busted lip and nose you gave me just now."

Janet started to cry. It was a combination relief/anger cry. Walt and I stayed silent while she let it run its course.

Then she quieted down and looked at me.

"Come inside and let me fix your face," she said.

"On that happy note, I'll be in my office awaiting reports and updates," Walt said. "You play nice, you crazy kids."

Janet turned to him.

"You're not off the hook, buster," she said.

"No, ma'am," Walt said. "Or is that yes, ma'am."

"Go away, Walt," I said. "And call me when you have something worth the price of a call. And take the goon squad with you."

"Jane?" Walt said.

"I'll talk to her later after I get some sleep."

Walt nodded, entered his wife's car, waited for his men to follow in their sedan and then he drove away.

Janet stood up and pointed to the open trailer door.

"Go!" she commanded.

"Yes, ma'am," I said.

"Yes, ma'am my ass, you stupid fool," Janet said.

I sat at my tiny kitchen table while Janet dragged out the first-aid kit from the bathroom and cleaned and dressed my cuts.

"Why do men always feel the need to fight?" she said as she washed out the mouse under my left eye. "Does it make them feel better about things?"

"Do I look like I'm feeling better right now?" I said.

"Hold still."

"Ouch," I said as the alcohol swab stung. "And I noticed you didn't have a problem using me for a punching bag."

"That's different."

"How?"

"I reacted out of stress."

"Hey, a punch in the mouth is a punch in the mouth."

"Don't change the subject."

"That is the subject."

Janet finished up, then sat in a chair and looked at me.

"If you were killed, I would be the one to tell Regan," she said. "You think about that and tell me you didn't deserve a punch in the mouth."

I didn't have to think about it to know the answer.

"Want to get some sleep or fool around?" Janet said.

"Both."

I woke up five hours later, grabbed my cell phone and a mug of coffee and slipped outside to call Jane.

"I was wondering when you'd call," Jane said.

"I need you to do something with me," I said.

"I've told you before, Bekker, I'm married," Jane said. "And five weeks pregnant to boot."

"Remember where Simms lives?" I said.

"Sure."

"Meet me there around six," I said.

"For?"

"I'll explain later," I said.

"Should I bring backup?"

"Only if they have donuts and coffee."

I hung up.

Behind me, Janet said, "Meet who where around six?"

"Sheriff Jane for an information exchange."

"I have to be on duty at eight," Janet said. "Want me to call out?"

I shook my head.

"I don't know how long I'll be," I said.

"What time should I tell the detectives to pick me up?"

"Five."

Janet nodded.

"That gives us enough time to eat an early dinner and burn off the calories with a little exercise."

"I could use a jog on the beach to loosen up the old bones," I said.

Janet shook her head as she wrapped her arms around my neck.

"Please tell me you aren't this stupid," she whispered in my ear.

CHAPTER 63

I slipped the key into the lock and opened the front door of Simms's villa. I entered and Jane followed me. I clicked on the lights in the living room and we stood in silence for a moment.

Each of us had a container of coffee.

We sipped.

"Mind telling me why we're here and what we're looking for," Jane said.

"Anything with Simms's DNA on it that your lab can process," I said.

"For?"

"Comparison to Jon Hughes's DNA."

Jane looked at me.

"Oh, God," she said.

"Best place would be her bathroom," I said. "Let's start there."

We entered the master bedroom, then the bathroom. I had a pocket full of zip-lock plastic bags and gave a few to Jane.

We found several hairbrushes with strands of hair in them and a spare razor which, while clean, was sure to have skin samples on the blade. Tubes of lipstick, a thermometer for taking body temperature, drinking glass on the sink, several different body scrub sponges in the shower and the prize, a toenail clipping behind the toilet.

"She must sit and clip," Jane said. "It's a woman thing."

"I think we have enough," I said.

I locked up and we returned to Jane's cruiser.

"Mind filling in the blanks and in-betweens now," Jane said as she drove us to the Public Safety Building.

"I don't have all the blanks just yet," I said. "Settle for the in-betweens?"

"I'll settle for what I can get," Jane said.

"The boys at Sacred Heart formed a little club born of anger and resentment," I said. "They hunt down and kill their mothers and videotape the event, maybe to relive the experience, maybe as proof to each other they were man enough to do it, I don't know. I'm sure Hughes had vital information to their little cause in his laptop and it's in the hands of whoever was the third person in the motel room that night."

"He was supposed to have sex with Simms and then kill her as an act of revenge for her abandoning him," Jane said. "And he couldn't or wouldn't and was killed for his trouble by said unknown third person. Jesus Christ, Bekker."

"This is about as far removed from Jesus Christ as you can get," I said.

"How do you build up that much hatred?" Jane said. "That you could seduce and murder your own mother."

"How do you seduce an entire country into believing it's the master race?" I said. "Or get four hundred people to drink poisoned Kool-Aid, or murder a pregnant actress to start a race war, or fly buildings into planes believing seventy-two virgins are on the other end of it?"

I lit a cigarette.

"Want one?" I said.

"I'd love one, but the mini-bun I have in the oven wouldn't," Jane said.

"I forgot. Sorry."

"No need," Jane said. "My idiot husband is the one who is sorry. I'm having him disabled."

I blew smoke and cocked an eye at Jane.

"Ouch," I said.

"I have my twenty-plus in, Jack," Jane said. "I can't raise another brat and do the job anymore. I'm too damn old now. I can handle one or the other, but not both."

"I'm sorry to hear that," I said. "You're a helluva cop in my book, for what that's worth."

"It's worth a lot," Jane said. "But not as much as being a helluva mother."

"When you pulling the pin?"

"Two weeks before the baby's due," Jane said. "I'll just fade away and never return. I have a senior deputy to take over until they can hold a special election."

We arrived at the Public Safety Building. Jane parked in her spot.

"I'll run this over to the lab," she said. "It will probably take twenty-four hours if they make it a priority. I'll make sure they do. I'll call you as soon as I have the results."

My car was parked next to Jane's cruiser.

"Smoking is out, is coffee?" I said.

"No, not yet."

"Drop off the evidence and let's get some."

"Be right back."

Twenty minutes later, we sat in a booth a nearby diner. We had coffee and slices of key lime pie. The pie was yellow with just the right mix of sweet and tart so that you tasted both without one dominating the other.

Jane forked a piece of pie into her mouth and washed it down with coffee.

"Get it off your chest, Jack," she said.

"This is what, number five for you?" I said.

Jane nodded. "My oldest is twenty-three. So what's on your mind?"

"What would it take for you to give up a baby?" I said.

Jane stared at me for a moment.

"I would die before I gave up a child of mine or allowed someone to take it away from me," she said.

"What if you were young, unmarried, broke, on drugs, afraid to tell your parents, any or all of the above and some I can't think of at the moment?" I said.

"You're not talking about me," Jane said. "You're talking about Simms."

"I'm trying to understand why a young woman would have a baby only to give it up for adoption when she doesn't have to have it at all," I said.

"Do you believe in abortion?" Jane said.

"No."

"Maybe Simms doesn't either," Jane said.

"Yeah, but it's easy for men to believe or not believe in something their body isn't capable of doing," I said. "It's different when a life is growing inside you and you're scared to death and all alone."

"You're not nearly as stupid as you look, are you, Jack," Jane said.

"I've been getting that a lot lately," I said. "I'm either getting better looking or smarter as I get older."

Jane grinned and ate another forkful of pie.

"What's really biting your bit?" she said.

"I think we both know Simms didn't kill Hughes," I said. "And that the lab will prove what we already suspect. I'm positive all charges against Simms will be dropped, especially if I find the actual killer. It will come out in open court for all to see that she was seduced by her own son for the purpose of revenge by this little boys club."

Jane nodded.

"I think I'd rather get the death penalty than live with

something like that," she said. "I think Simms will, too."

I nodded.

"Do you see any way this goes down without having that little tidbit come to light?" I said.

"No."

"Neither do I," I said.

"So what are you going to do, Bekker?" Jane said. "Any way this plays out, Simms is a ruined woman. It's better to be a free ruined woman than one sitting out her days on death row."

"Is it?" I said.

"When I was a little girl, my mother told me the sins we plant in our youth generally come to harvest when we're adults," Jane said.

"Your mother is a smart woman," I said.

"I'll be forty-six when this baby is born," Jane said. "Too bad she didn't teach me about birth control instead."

CHAPTER 64

"I've defended the worst element human beings have to offer in my career as a criminal attorney," David Clark said from behind his desk. "Mobsters, professional murderers, drug dealers and mob bosses like Eddie Crist. I can honestly say that I've never heard of such a scheme as this one. Orphaned boys plotting revenge against the women who abandoned them."

"It's her ticket to freedom," I said.

"Followed by a ticket to suicide," Clark said.

"She's not the type," I said.

"Who ever is?" Clark said. "A couple, three years ago, I was helping my wife with some yard work on a spring afternoon. My neighbor, his name was Tom, he came over to help us plant some rose bushes. My wife made some lemonade. We sat in the shade of the gazebo, drank the lemonade and told jokes. When we finished planting the rose bushes, Tom went home and hung himself in his living room while his wife was out shopping for a new pair of shoes to wear to their son's upcoming wedding. He never even left a note. I remember thinking afterward that Tom just wasn't the type."

"Not Simms," I said. "She'll disappear, go into hiding, maybe clerk for some firm down the road, but she won't take that way out."

"No?" Clark said. "Then why are we having this discussion if you're not concerned?"

"When will you see the judge?" I said.

"When are you available to present new evidence?"

"The DNA testing should be in tomorrow," I said. "Schedule for the first of next week. That gives me time to prepare notes and statements."

Clark nodded.

"What about potential suspects?" he said. "Any idea who was behind kidnapping you?"

"Yeah, the same man behind the murders."

"The kid you . . . killed? What do we know about him?"

"Nothing at the moment. Awaiting an ID from Walt," I said. "He's just a pawn."

Clark nodded again. "I'll call the judge."

I stood up from my chair. "And I'll call you with an update in a few days."

"Wait a minute," Clark said. "You're up to something. What?"

"Theories and speculation," I said.

"I don't buy that," Clark said. "This is my case, Bekker. You stuck me with it, but I'm in it to win it, so don't hold back."

"I'm not and I won't," I said. "See you in a few days."

I rode the elevator to the street and lit a fresh cigarette. As I walked to the lot my car was parked in, my cell phone rang. I checked the incoming number. It was Walt.

"Got an ID on the kid for you," he said. "Name is Jeff Weaver. He was dumped in Sacred Heart when he was eleven. Want details?"

"No."

"I didn't think so. You talk to Jane?"

"Yes."

"Keep me up to snuff."

"Sure."

I dropped the phone into my pocket and walked to my car. It wasn't that I didn't want details of Jeff Weaver's life, it's just easier not knowing too much about a life you just ended.

261

Not that it's ever easy when you are forced to take a life. It isn't. Even when the man is trying to kill you, there is still a certain amount of regret at ending something that doesn't belong to you. At least, it's that way for me.

In the case of Jeff Weaver, I didn't want to know.

Not now.

Maybe later.

When I'd finished what I started.

Chapter 65

My plane touched down in Provo, Utah, at eight minutes past midnight. It wasn't a busy night at the airport and we taxied quickly from runway to gate in a matter of minutes.

My luggage was a paperback book I didn't read. I skirted baggage claim and went directly to the cabstand on the street outside the terminal. I tossed the book into a trash bin on the curb.

I opened a new pack of cigarettes and lit one off a paper match. I wasn't twenty-five feet from the revolving doors and caught a dirty look from a woman exiting through them.

I ignored her and pulled out my cell phone. I searched through the memory bank and hit enter for Paul Lawrence's private cell number.

It was two hours earlier in Washington. Paul answered on the second ring.

"Special Agent Lawrence. The Wizards are beating the Knicks in the fourth quarter, so this better be good," he said.

"Paul, John Bekker," I said.

"Hey, Jack. What's going on you're calling this late?"

"How long will it take you to fire up one of those FBI jets of yours and fly to Utah?" I said.

"Three hours door-to-door. Why?"

"I was just wondering if you feel like making a federal arrest," I said. "The kind that would make you a household name at the Washington parties you get invited to."

"I'm home alone watching a losing team play another losing team," Lawrence said. "That's about the extent of my party circuit."

"Get a federal search warrant and call me when you land in Provo," I said.

"John, federal warrants don't come easy," Lawrence said. "I wake a federal judge up, he's going to be really pissed off if I don't have a damn good reason."

"You have one," I said.

"Well, give it to me then so we both know what it is."

After I hung up with Lawrence, I tossed the spent cigarette to the curb and lit another. I felt a twinge of guilt leaving Janet's vapor tubes at home, but I figured I could live with it for the time being.

What I couldn't live with were death threats to my family or me and a woman getting the death penalty for sins unrelated to a crime she didn't commit.

Thirty-seven minutes later, a yellow cab let me off on the street adjacent to the TRAX Corporation parking lot. The driver asked me if he should wait. I told him no, and gave him a crisp fifty-dollar bill for his trouble.

I waited for the cab to speed away, then I cupped my hand to hide the flame of the match and lit a cigarette.

I smoked in silence, in the dark, and waited.

I didn't have to wait long.

Sal Meeks approached on foot from the corner. He came into the pale light of the parking lot lights, half of which were lit for night use.

It was a cool night and Meeks wore a trench coat with the buttons closed and the belt tied. The collar was up around his neck.

"Are you sure about this, Mr. Bekker?" he said when he approached me.

"Yes."

"Then we should call the police."

"I have the FBI on the way," I said. "It would take a month to explain this to the local PD. Besides, it crosses state lines, which makes it federal."

Meeks nodded.

"What do you want me to do?" he said.

"It's just one other guard on duty?"

Meeks nodded again.

"Okay, let's go then," I said.

We entered the parking lot and walked across the pavement to the revolving doors that fed into the lobby. They were locked after midnight. So was the standard glass door adjacent to the revolving doors, but Meeks had the key.

He unlocked the door and we entered.

Immediately, the kid behind the security desk jumped to his feet.

"His name is James," Meeks said softly.

Meeks and I crossed the wide lobby to the desk. Our footsteps echoed loudly on the highly polished, tiled floor.

"Mr. Meeks, what are you . . . ?" James said.

Meeks held up his right hand to silence James.

"James, this is very important," Meeks said. "Where is Josh?"

"Making rounds, Mr. Meeks," James said.

"How long does that take and when did he leave?" I said.

James looked at his watch. "Ten minutes ago and it takes around thirty minutes for a complete loop."

"What's the last stop on the rounds before returning to the desk?" I said.

"The basement parking garage," James said. "It's closed in summer, but it's still on the rounds."

"How do you get in from here?" I said.

James pointed to a shiny steel door a few feet to the left of the security desk.

"Is it locked?"

"Yeah."

"Is there another way out?"

"The roll-up doors, but they're locked up tight for the summer."

I pointed to the steel door.

"Open it."

James went to the door and fished out a brass key from his key ring.

I turned to Meeks. "If I'm not back in thirty minutes, call 911 and FBI Agent Paul Lawrence," I said as I gave Meeks my cell phone. "His number is in the saved file."

Meeks took the phone and nodded.

"James, lock the door behind me and don't open it unless you hear my voice only on the other side," I said. "Understand? No one else but me."

"Yes."

I opened the door.

"Lock it behind me," I said, then entered the landing and closed the door.

The stairwell was lit by wall lamps, but still dark. I walked down to the garage. The emergency lighting was enough to see by, but barely. The interior was all shadows and dark corners.

It was large enough for two hundred cars.

A steel door exactly like the one in the lobby was adjacent to the elevator. I walked to the door, turned and took a position behind an iron support beam about six feet away that went from floor to ceiling.

I stood there for twenty minutes.

I tried not to think of anything and focus on the task at hand. The slightest distraction can throw you off your game. Like a hitter at the plate ignoring fifty thousand screaming fans, if he hears the fans and lets them in, focus on putting bat to ball is compromised.

Most people know about night vision, how if you stand in darkness long enough your eyes adjust and you can see better. It's like that with your hearing, too. Stand still in total silence long enough and your hearing grows more acute to the point you really can hear a pin drop on a hard floor.

I didn't hear a pin drop.

I did hear footsteps behind the steel door. Then a key in a lock.

I sucked in air and let it out through my nose.

The door opened slowly. Josh emerged from behind it and walked toward the wall on his right.

I removed my jacket and let it silently drop to the floor.

Josh held a small electronic reader in his right hand. He ran the device over a wall-mounted electric eye to take a reading of his patrol time. When he turned around, I emerged from the shadows and stood about ten feet in front of him.

There was a split second before recognition showed in his eyes.

Josh smiled. It wasn't the boyish grin of earlier. Cast in shadows, Josh's face was hard and deep. The smile told the story of arrogance and defiance. It was a fuck-you smile.

"I should have killed you when I had the chance," he said.

"The night is still young," I said. "You'll have your chance."

Josh snorted a laugh.

"Oh, I may be a few decades older than you, and you may be a black belt in karate, but if you want to know if I can kill you or not, the answer is yes," I said. "I can."

"Prove it," Josh said.

"Don't make me, Josh. I'd rather not have to," I said. "Enough people have died over this stupid game."

"Stupid game?" Josh said in a sudden burst of anger.

"Murdering women because they gave their sons up for adoption, what else would you call it?" I said.

"Justice."

"For what?" I said. "Putting a child up for adoption is legal. Murder is not."

"What do you know about it?" Josh said. "You probably grew up in a nice warm home somewhere with two parents, a dog and a white picket fence. Do you know what it feels like to be a little kid and wonder who the fuck you are? Why Mommy didn't want you? What you did wrong to get dumped in an orphanage with all the other loser assholes?"

"So what?" I said. "Everybody has something they have to live with, Josh. It's called life. My wife was murdered and my daughter watched it happen. She grew up a vegetable. Who had the better childhood, you or her?"

"At least she had parents," Josh said. "At least she has a name and knows where her blood comes from."

"You don't get it and I guess whoever brainwashed you with this garbage knew what they were doing," I said.

"Look, Mr. Bekker, I don't want to kill you, but I will if you don't get out of my way and leave me alone," Josh said.

"I can't do that, Josh," I said. "You know that. Besides, I can prove that Jon Hughes wasn't killed by Simms and put the FBI on you and your boys club. Maybe you don't think you left evidence behind when you killed Hughes or the others, but you did. A single strand of hair with your DNA is enough to convict you and send you to prison for life. Do you want that or do you want to make a deal for your freedom?"

"What deal?"

"I know you're not the brains behind this little operation," I said. "Which one of your former Sacred Heart roommates is?"

"I don't have to tell you shit," Josh said. "Seeing as how in another minute, you'll be dead and you won't matter."

"You're just the enforcer, aren't you, Josh?" I said. "You go along to make sure they do what they're supposed to do, have sex with their mothers, film the event and then kill them. If they back out, get cold feet, you step in and kill them both. Isn't that how it works, Josh?"

Josh grinned at me.

I took his grin as a yes.

"That night in the motel you got cold waiting around and turned up the heat," I said. "You waited in the tub for them to come in. Then you really fucked up when you body-slammed Hughes into the wall and woke up the neighbors. You're not getting off, Josh, so what do you say to that deal?"

His eyes told the story.

You can see the crazy in a person's eyes if you choose to look. Crazed maniacs all have that same appearance in their eyes that raises a red flag and telegraphs their intent. Compare Hitler's eyes to Manson's and you'll see what I mean. The lights are on, but no one's home.

"I say go fuck yourself," Josh said.

The eyes never lie.

The kid was insane.

His lights were on, but he'd checked out.

"So at least tell me what happened," I said. "Hughes get cold feet? He couldn't bring himself to finish what he started, so you interjected yourself into the mix and killed him for his trouble. Then what happened? Why didn't you kill Simms?"

"Why do you care?"

"If you're going to kill me anyway, what does it matter if I know?" I said.

"Okay, I'll tell you," Josh said. "The stupid bitch passed out cold. I waited for her to wake up, but the best I could do was open her eyes for a few seconds at a time. So what I did, I sat her on top of him, placed the letter opener in her hands and stabbed old Jon through the heart. I was gonna kill her, but she didn't wake up. What's the fun in killing someone for revenge if they don't know about it? The cops came and I beat it out the window. Any more fucking questions?"

"Just one," I said. "Where's the evidence hidden? The laptop and video camera?"

"I guess that one will just have to remain a secret," Josh said.

"The FBI is on the way, Josh," I said. "I'd prefer to do this quietly."

Josh tossed the scanner in his right hand to the ground.

"I'll tell the police you attacked me in the dark," he said. "I didn't want to kill you, but you gave me no choice."

"I don't want to do this, Josh," I said.

Josh took a few steps toward me.

"We don't always get what we want, do we?" he said. "Mr. Bekker," he added.

The way to fight a trained karate expert is to neutralize their weapons. Kicks from a distance, punches and blocks from in close, counterpunches and holds—take away those and you're fighting just a regular Joe.

Of course, while you're doing that, you could just wind up with a broken neck and dead on the floor.

Josh grinned as he spun into a lazy feeling-out kick that I easily sidestepped.

He landed with the grace of a gazelle and immediately lashed out with a straight right leg kick that I jumped backward from just as it made contact with my chest.

"You're pretty spry," Josh said. "For an old man."

I rushed in and launched a three-punch combination, of which all three found a home on Josh's face.

Caught off guard, Josh backed up.

Satisfied I'd captured his attention, I jumped backward to safety.

Josh laughed and spit a tiny drop of blood.

"That was pretty good," he said. "Can you do that again?"

"What do you think?"

"I don't think so."

"Let's find out."

Josh came in spinning on the ball of his right foot and came out of the spin with a high kick to my head.

I timed the kick and moved, but I was off a hair and the toe of his shoe caught me in the temple.

I fell sideways a bit and gave him an opening.

Josh swept my legs out from under me with a toe sweep and I landed hard on the cement floor.

Josh went up and came down with a left heel kick that, if it had landed, would have done considerable damage to my face.

I rolled out of the way and rolled five more times for good measure.

"Get up, old man," Josh said. "Get up."

I got up.

Josh moved in with four successive leg kicks.

I backed up three times. On the fourth leg kick, I rushed in and allowed the kick to hit me in the chest. At the same time I let fly with a roundhouse right that caught Josh flush on the jaw.

The kick knocked me backward.

My punch knocked Josh almost to the floor.

He righted himself against an iron support beam.

"Hurt, don't it?" I said.

Josh spit a mouthful of blood.

"I'm gonna make you fucking beg me to kill you," he said.

Take away the kick and you take away the weapon.

Easier said than done.

Most things are.

I moved in and took a kick to the chest, immediately followed by a second kick to the left side of my face.

I stumbled backward, ate the pain and tasted the blood.

Josh moved forward and lashed out with a straight right leg kick.

I covered up like a boxer, peek-a-boo style.

My elbows absorbed the blow.

Josh rushed in and launched a dozen punches at me. Most hit my elbows and forearms, one or two found their way to my face.

I went low and pounded his midsection with a series of lefts and rights until he backed up several feet. Then I let fly with a left hook to his jaw that sent Josh reeling backward into an iron support beam.

He hit the beam hard, doubled over in pain for a moment, then, like a wounded animal, launched another attack as a means of defense. A wounded cat is a dangerous cat.

I jumped backward as Josh rushed me low and took me down at the legs in a mixed martial arts move.

I landed on my back with Josh on my legs.

He punched down at me.

I covered my face with my arms.

The thing about punching downward without the leverage of your legs is that there isn't much power generated. If you've ever watched one of those cage matches where one fighter is on the mat and the other is raining blows down on him, more often than not, neither man is seriously hurt when they stand up.

"You motherfucker!" Josh screamed as he threw punch after punch.

I went into a turtle-shell defense to protect my face.

"You fucking motherfucker!" Josh screamed as he continued to throw punches.

My wrists and elbows were getting bruised and banged up, but most of the punches hadn't reached their mark.

I waited for an opening, saw it and timed his punches so that I grabbed both of Josh's wrists in my hands.

There was a second of surprise on his face.

Like he said, I'm pretty spry for an old man.

Then I yanked him forward and smashed my forehead into his face.

The sound was not unlike a ripe melon being dropped.

Blood from his nose squirted on my face.

Josh rolled off me to the floor.

I rolled in the opposite direction.

Slowly, I stood up.

I waited.

It took him a while for his vision to clear and the bells in his head to stop ringing. Then he made his way up and onto weak and wobbly legs.

I launched three stiff jabs to Josh's busted and bleeding nose that backed him up and then I caved him in with a left hook to his midsection.

Josh doubled over.

I straightened him up with a right knee to his jaw and followed that up with a right hook to his face.

Josh struck the iron support beam again. I rushed in and threw body blows at his exposed midsection.

He finally caved in again and I straightened him up with a left uppercut that bounced his head off the support beam.

He was done.

I finished the job with another head butt to his face. Josh was unconscious before he hit the floor.

I stepped back and gasped for air.

My lungs were on fire.

Battery acid ran through my veins.

I wanted to kill this son of a bitch in the worst way.

I didn't.

I would have to look my daughter in the eye, and her opinion of me prevented me from cold-blooded murder.

My breathing slowed.

My head cleared.

Common sense prevailed.

I took a step back and thanked Regan for being in my heart.

Adrenaline prevented my hands and face from hurting. I knew that when it wore off, I would be feeling this for weeks.

I knelt down, removed the belt from around his waist, and used it to tie Josh's hands behind his back. If he woke up before the ambulance arrived, he would be going nowhere.

I walked up the stairs and banged on the door.

"Meeks, it's Bekker!" I shouted. "Open the door."

The door opened and I stepped out to the lobby.

Meeks and James looked at me.

"Jesus Christ," Meeks said.

James peeked past me at the open door.

"Better go down and sit with him," I said.

James looked his question at me.

"He can't hurt you," I said. "Or anybody else."

James nodded.

"Are you . . . okay?" Meeks said.

"Yeah. Is there a bathroom in the lobby?" I said.

James pointed toward the elevators. There was a door marked Restrooms.

"Call 911 on my phone and request an ambulance," I said. "I'm going to the men's room and throw up. I'll be right back."

CHAPTER 66

One of the perks of being a member of the rank and file inside the FBI is you don't need a rental car when flying for business. Paul Lawrence called ahead and had a Bureau sedan waiting for him at the airport.

He drove from the airport to the TRAX Corporation where I met him on the sidewalk outside the lobby.

I was smoking a cigarette when he arrived.

Or trying to in between paper towel wipes of blood from my lips.

Paul got out of the sedan and stood next to me in the light.

"How's the other guy?" he said.

"On his way to the hospital," I said. "I told the paramedics he's wanted for murder by the FBI and you'd be along in a while to arrest him. In the meantime, a pair of locals will babysit him."

"What about you?" Lawrence said. "You look like you could use a hospital yourself."

"What I could use is lots of little drinks all lined up in a row," I said. "But I'll settle for coffee on the ride."

"Ride where?" Lawrence said. "It's two in the morning."

I opened the passenger door of the sedan.

"You coming?" I said.

Sacred Heart was locked up tighter than a wet snare drum when we arrived at the front gates.

A security guard in the guard shack came to the gate to greet us.

"Gates open at eight," the guard said.

Lawrence flashed his FBI identification. "Today they open early."

Brother Philip occupied a small home behind the exercise yard. A well-kept garden in front was in full bloom. I could smell flowers on the night air, but I couldn't identify them.

A security guard on patrol escorted us to the front door.

"He ain't gonna like this," the guard said.

"I really don't care what he likes," I said.

Lawrence leaned on the doorbell until lights inside the house came on and we heard footsteps.

Lawrence released the bell.

The door opened a crack.

Wearing a robe over pajamas, Brother Philip peered through the crack and his eyes went wide at the sight of my face.

"You should see the other guy," I said. "His name is Josh Andrus and by now he's safely in the arms of the police."

Lawrence displayed his identification and the federal warrant.

"Philip Lewis Anderson, you're under arrest for conspiracy to commit murder and for inciting the murders of Jon Hughes, Scott Lind, Thomas Sutton, Robert Maggio and Stephen Stousser," Lawrence said. "And I'll think of some other shit later."

"Will you allow me to get dressed?" Brother Philip said, without a hint of denial at the charges.

Lawrence and I escorted him to his bedroom where Brother Philip changed.

"Why?" I said as he tied his shoes.

"There's only so many broken spirits one man can endure," Brother Philip said. "After a while you realize the pain has to go somewhere."

"So you started a little cult and recruited the weakest ones and convinced them murdering Mommy was the only way to self-respect and manhood?" I said.

"I don't expect you to understand," Brother Philip said.

Lawrence removed handcuffs from his pocket.

"I hope you enjoy tiny little spaces," Lawrence said. "You'll be living in one for the next thirty years to life."

Chapter 67

I flew to Washington with Paul Lawrence on the FBI jet. We had breakfast and discussed Brother Philip's written and recorded statements.

He started his little brotherhood about twelve years ago when, as he put it, he could no longer endure the broken spirits of so many young boys anymore. He recruited the weakest boys who he knew would have no chance at life after leaving Sacred Heart for the purpose of giving them self-confidence and giving their lives meaning. It became obvious after a while that the only way to do that was to allow the boys to decide what was the best course to follow to achieve that goal. Revenge against their mothers, the women who bore them and then abandoned them, was the logical choice. Brother Philip had the means to locate the women. The boys decided upon the method. In all, thirteen women were murdered at the hands of their sons. Most engaged in sexual relations with them prior to being murdered. A final act of humiliation for their sins. Jon Hughes came up with the idea of recording the murders for others to watch as a recruitment tool, sort of an incentive to join the party. Josh Andrus served as enforcer. Those who failed in their mission needed to be removed from the program to protect the secrecy of the operation.

Lawrence and I sipped coffee as the jet made its approach to the airport.

"Anderson is certifiable," Lawrence said. "This is going to be one long-ass process to convict. We might have to settle for a lifetime stay in a mental hospital."

I nodded.

"Thirty years at the puzzle factory is no cake walk," I said. "And the Andrus kid will be a very old man before he sees daylight, if ever."

"I have to go to the office when we land," Lawrence said. "Want a ride home?"

"Just me on your fancy jet," I said. "Think of the taxpayers."

"I don't think the taxpayers will mind this once," Lawrence said.

CHAPTER 68

"This one will need stitches," Janet said as she cleaned and dressed the cuts and bruises on my face. "And what the hell happened to your hands?"

"What one needs stitches?" I said. "And what happened to my hands is what happens when bone meets bone bare-knuckled."

"That melon-shaped split in your forehead," Janet said.

"Oh."

"Want to tell me about it?"

"Let me reload on the coffee and have a smoke first," I said.

Janet stitched.

I sipped, smoked and talked.

When Janet was finished stitching, I was finished talking.

She took Oz's rusty lawn chair beside mine. We listened to the tide roll in and the waves break on the beach. Gulls flapped around and screeched at each other in their never-ending battle for scraps.

"I suppose I should be proud of you," Janet said. "Breaking a major case, proving Simms innocent and locking up the guilty all in one fell swoop."

"But?"

"I feel like I'm losing you," Janet said. "You're becoming addicted to this adrenaline rush your job provides and I'm afraid that you will find married life . . . well, boring."

"My face could use a little boring right about now," I said.

"You say that now," Janet said. "What about later when your cuts are healed and that need for an adrenaline rush kicks in?"

"Try me."

"I will," Janet said and stood up. She extended her right hand into mine. "If you're not feeling too old right about now."

I stood up.

"You know what they say," I said. "You're only as old as the woman you feel."

Janet opened the door to my trailer.

"Start feeling young, big boy," she said.

We lazed around in bed the rest of the afternoon until I fell asleep with my head on Janet's chest. When I awoke, I was alone and it was dark outside my tiny bedroom window.

The sound of pots and pans rattling around told me Janet hadn't left. I went to the kitchen to investigate. She was at the sink, washing pans, and turned to look at me.

"Coffee's fresh, dinner's in the oven," she said.

"The oven works?" I said.

"It's old, but works just fine," Janet said. "Kind of like its owner."

I filled a mug and took a seat at the table.

Janet took a seat opposite me.

"So what now and how will you explain that face of yours to Regan?" she said.

"Tomorrow's what now is a meeting with Clark, the judge and prosecutors," I said. "And after they file charges and indict Anderson, Josh Andrus and I'm sure a host of others, I'll take a trip to Florida to see Simms."

"Is that necessary?" Janet said. "Won't a phone call do?"

"It's necessary and then that's the end of it," I said.

"Why can't you rescue a homely girl from time to time," Janet said. "They're out there if you look hard enough."

"I'll ignore that and move on to part two of your question," I said. "By the time I go to Florida, my face will be reasonably normal. I'd like to take you, Regan and Mark with me for a little R&R, if you can take a few days off, of course."

"Every time I get mad at you, you say the right thing," Janet said.

"It's a bad habit of mine," I said.

"Want to eat in here or outside?"

"Outside."

I made a fire in the wire trashcan. We ate with the light and warmth on our faces and listened to the breaking waves we couldn't see in the dark background.

We didn't talk.

No need to.

Nights don't get much better than that.

CHAPTER 69

I met up with Walt and Jane in the lobby of Clark's downtown office building.

"Did I tell you you're the best cop ever born?" Walt said. "And also the stupidest and possibly the ugliest at the moment."

"It's impossible to be the best and the stupidest at something at the same time," Jane said. "It's like that jumbo shrimp thing."

"Don't forget ugly," I said.

"He's got you on that one, I'm afraid," Jane said.

Clark was expecting us and had the conference room set up for breakfast. The surprise guest was Paul Lawrence.

Seated at the conference table, Lawrence stood up and shook Walt's hand.

"Been a while, Walt," Lawrence said.

"Too long," Walt said.

"How's Elizabeth?" Lawrence said.

"Mean as a snake and twice as deadly."

"Paul, have you met Sheriff Jane Morgan?" I said.

Lawrence extended his right hand to Jane.

"Ten, twelve years ago when I was still with the local division," Lawrence said. "How are you?"

"Better now that morning sickness has worn off," Jane said.

"Congratulations," Lawrence said.

"To all of us," Clark said. "Shall we have breakfast and discuss our plan of attack for court?"

We ate a catered breakfast at the table. Somebody knew how to make scrambled eggs the way they were meant to be eaten.

Lawrence produced Jon Hughes's laptop and set it on the table.

"Names, dates, plots, victims and videos," Lawrence said. "It's all there. Enough to send Anderson away for life with Andrus as a cellmate. We recovered it at Anderson's home on the Sacred Heart grounds, along with his own files from his PC. There are a dozen other new recruits on the grounds and several others scattered around the country. The new recruits will be relocated to new homes where they will receive therapy for as long as necessary."

"I anticipate a slam dunk in court this afternoon when we meet with the judge," Clark said. "Total exoneration for Simms, indictments for Anderson, Andrus and the others. Congratulations, Bekker, it's all your doing."

I made eye contact with Walt and Jane.

"I know what you're thinking," Clark said. "Her career and reputation are ruined. Both can be repaired over time, but not from the inside of a prison cell awaiting the death penalty. As a prosecutor, she knows and understands how things work."

I ate a cinnamon bun.

"I'm flying down to Palm Beach to talk to Simms and answer any questions she has," I said. "I booked a flight for day after tomorrow."

"I won't be able to get away," Clark said. "The paperwork on this alone will take a week."

"She'll probably fly home right after I talk to her," I said. "God knows, she and Campbell Crist must be sick of each other by now."

Clark nodded.

"I'll see to your bill and expenses," he said. "And a bonus if she can afford one."

"My expenses are covered," I said. "No hurry on anything else."

The afternoon in court passed slowly. Clark explained his case and evidence to the judge in chambers and Lawrence and I made statements in detail. Lawrence played evidence from the laptop to the judge. It was enough to make you sick to your stomach.

Clark requested all charges against Simms be dropped.

The judge agreed.

Lawrence requested federal indictments be brought forth against Philip Anderson and Josh Andrus and others named in the sordid details of Lawrence's report.

The judge agreed.

I left the courtroom with Walt, Clark and Jane.

The judge and Lawrence stayed behind to decide upon a federal location for a grand jury indictment.

"And that's the way it goes sometimes," Walt said as we walked along the street.

CHAPTER 70

The Crist Villa in Palm Beach, Florida, occupied six acres of prime real estate overlooking the beach. It had six bedrooms and fifteen rooms total. A fourteen-foot high, pink stucco fence surrounded the property. Palm trees and coconuts were everywhere. Eddie Crist built the place for privacy and it was impossible to see inside the compound from street level.

Security was tight. Campbell took six bodyguards for protection. Closed-circuit television cameras scanned and recorded every square inch of the property. I heard that when he was alive, Eddie Crist used the villa as a meeting place for crime bosses from around the country. They would line up beach chairs in the sand by the beach and plot their business right under the noses of the feds, all the while catching a tan.

A bodyguard saw me in. He didn't bother to pat me down. Most if not all of the security staff knew me on a first-name basis by now.

Simms and Campbell Crist were tanning poolside in the massive backyard. They were smoking cigarettes and sipping iced tea when I came out the sliding doors and approached them.

For once, both women wore the tops of their bikinis.

Simms had almost as deep a tan as Campbell.

"Hi, Jack," Simms said. "Thanks for coming."

"Nice to see you again, Bekker," Campbell said.

"Want an iced tea?" Simms said.

I took a chair beside Simms. "Sure."

Simms got up to pour a tall glass of tea over crushed ice. She handed me the glass and reclaimed her chair.

"I talked to Clark for several hours this morning," she said.

I nodded.

"My reputation and career are ruined."

I nodded again.

Simms misted up a bit as she said, "But at least I know I didn't kill . . . him."

Campbell rolled her eyes as she reached for the box of tissues on the table beside her and tossed it to Simms.

"Well, for God's sake, don't cry about it," Campbell said.

Simms removed a tissue and dabbed her eyes.

"Want to tell me about Jon Hughes?" I said.

Campbell stood up. "I've already heard this part," she said and walked into the villa.

"I'd just graduated college," Simms said. "I was starting law school in the fall. There was a frat party. I'm Catholic. I contacted Catholic Charities and they found a home for my . . . son with a nice young couple who couldn't conceive. I never knew they were killed in a car accident and he was placed at Sacred Heart."

"Why would you?" I said. "Secrecy is part of the adoption process, isn't it?"

Simms looked away for a moment and used another tissue to wipe her eyes.

"Oh God, Bekker," she said. "I was seduced by my own son."

I let her cry for a while. When she blew her nose and settled down, I lit two cigarettes and gave her one.

"This won't help right now, but remember this one thing," I said. "You're the real victim in this mess."

Simms nodded and wiped her eyes.

"And that makes me feel better how?" she said.

"It doesn't," I said. "Only time and understanding will.

Enough time goes by and understanding leads to acceptance. I know something about that."

Simms stared at me for a while.

"I guess you do," she said.

"Stay down here for a while, think things over and let me know what you want to do," I said. "I can always fly down or drive and take you home."

"That won't be necessary," Campbell said from behind me. "I can make those arrangements, Bekker, don't worry."

"Sure," I said and stood up. "Well, I have to be somewhere. I'll talk to you soon."

Simms nodded and pulled a fresh tissue from the box.

"I'll walk you out," Campbell said and looked at Simms. "And you man up, for God's sake."

I walked with Campbell to the side gate of the fence. She opened the gate and we walked to the front of the villa where my rental car was parked.

Campbell handed me a folded check.

It was for fifty thousand dollars.

"What's this?" I said.

"It's called money, Mr. Bekker," Campbell said. "And you earned every penny of it judging by your face."

"You're paying her bills?" I said.

Campbell stared at me for a moment.

"Umm, how shall I put this?" she said. "You see, Bekker, Carly and I . . . we found each other. We're . . . well, we love each other. We're good for each other. I think we'll be together for a long time. What more can I say about it?"

"I'm glad," I said. "Happy for you both."

"Really?"

"Yeah, really."

Campbell kissed me on the cheek and watched as I drove off.

As Walt said, that's the way it goes sometimes.

CHAPTER 71

I arrived at the motel near the beach fifteen minutes after leaving the Crist mansion. Janet and Regan were poolside. Mark was in the pool, splashing some kid his own age with one of those giant water guns.

Molly was on Regan's lap, taking a snooze as Regan stroked the cat's neck and ears. Regan had insisted we bring Molly and we had to settle for a small motel that allowed pets rather than a large hotel on the main drag.

Nobody seemed to mind, especially Molly.

Regan looked at me as I took a chair next to her and Janet.

"Okay?" Regan said.

She still didn't speak much, just an occasional word or two.

It's enough for now.

Maybe someday I'll tell her how her place in my heart prevented murder.

"Yeah, okay," I said.

Regan smiled at me. Even Molly raised her head to look up and see what was going on. She quickly lost interest and returned to snoozing.

"You left your cell phone," Janet said. "That lawyer David Clark called. He wants to talk to you about taking on some new work. It appears he's even more of a celebrity and is besieged with new clients of the shady kind."

"What did you tell him?" I said.

"That you're officially retired."

I looked at Janet.

"You are officially retired, aren't you?" Janet said.

I looked at my daughter.

She gave me a tiny head nod.

I stood up.

"Let's go have some fun," I said.

ABOUT THE AUTHOR

Al Lamanda is the author of the mystery/thriller novels *Dunston Falls, Walking Homeless, Running Homeless* and *Sunset.* He has also written several screenplays. A native of New York City, he is presently working on his latest novel.